ACCIDENTAL
EYEWITNESS

*When a killer thinks there
isn't a shred of evidence to be found,
there might be an accidental witness.*

Also by Alice Zogg

Stand-Alone Mystery
A Bet Turned Deadly

R. A. Huber Mysteries

Evil at Shore Haven
Guilty or Not
Murder at the Cubbyhole
Revamp Camp
Final Stop Albuquerque
The Fall of Optimum House
The Lonesome Autocrat
Tracking Backward
Turn the Joker Around
Reaching Checkmate

ACCIDENTAL
EYEWITNESS

ALICE ZOGG

aventine press

This book is a work of fiction.

Published by Aventine Press
55 East Emerson St.
Chula Vista CA 91911
www.aventinepress.com

ISBN: 978-1-59330-932-9

Library of Congress Control Number: 2017912216
Library of Congress Cataloging-in-Publication Data
Accidental Eyewitness/Alice Zogg
Printed in the United States of America

In memory of my friend Edith,
who loved snorkeling near tropical islands

CREDITS

Credit is due to Jackie Houchin, who explained the function of rescue inhalers for people suffering from asthma. She was even so kind as to let me borrow one. Rosemary Lord described a full-blown, life-or-death sort of asthma attack to me. Thank you, Rosemary, for sharing your painful experience which you would prefer to forget. Thanks are also in order to my son-in-law Sam Levering, who refreshed my memory about scuba diving and snorkeling. Again, I counted on my daughter Franziska for proofreading the manuscript. It is a tedious task, but she does it to perfection. Gayle Bartos-Pool deserves credit for an excellent editing job. My gratitude goes out to the members of the Los Angeles chapter of Sisters in Crime. Their support and friendship keeps me on track. When doing research for previous books, my husband, Wilfried, accompanied me when scouting out locations. Since *Isle of Ease* does not exist and is entirely a place of my imagination, he was off the hook with this work.

THE PLANNING

One morning in the month of February, a person sat at breakfast somewhere in Southern California, staring into space. No one would have imagined that beneath the stoic façade of this law-abiding citizen, murder was being plotted. Yet that was exactly what went on in the individual's mind. Not that any facial expression would have mattered; he or she was alone. The planning was precise, down to every exacting detail. The wicked human even thought up a plan B, should there be unpredictable circumstances to ruin the ploy. With a slight nod, the person thought, yes, it will work like a charm, and with any luck, go down as accidental death. On the off chance that there would be a homicide investigation, there is no way the crime can be fixed on me.

The planner hesitated for a second. Is it worth the risk? What risk? There is none, in fact. No evidence leading to me will exist. Do I really want to go through with this? Sure as hell I do! The schemer went in search of pen and paper, wrote the entire plot down - - memorizing each aspect - - and then fed the lines into the shredder.

CHAPTER 1

Kurt Nobel, known as "The Real Estate King," was ruthless in business yet generous with people in his personal life. For those who dared cross him, there was hell to pay. Physically, he was 54, six feet tall and in good shape, well-groomed, with brown hair graying at the temples and thinning on top.

At the moment, he watched his new young wife as she brushed her long, silky, blond hair in front of the vanity mirror. Absent minded, she had failed to notice him enter their bedroom. He stood, watching her composed movements.

Then he approached, addressing her image in the mirror and said, "What's going on in that aloof head of yours?"

Barbie replied, "I read the guest list and have a question."

"Feel free to add more of your friends."

"No, Hope is the only one I care to invite."

"What is it, then?"

She took a moment before voicing her objection. Finally, she asked, "Why do you want your former fiancée to come?"

"Oh, that's what's eating you! I want to show Alexa that there are no hard feelings, is all."

Barbie put her brush down and turned away from the mirror. Facing him, she stated, "I believe that deep down you're still in love with her, whether you know it or not."

"Alexa and I were done years ago. Are you that insecure?"

"Insecurity has nothing to do with it. I think it is a mistake to invite the Wellers."

"You're too late, my gorgeous worrywart; I've already mailed out the invitations." That said, he kissed her on the forehead and left her to finish getting dressed for their dinner engagement that evening.

In order to get her mind off Alexa, Barbie cheered herself up by imagining what fun it would be to spend a week in the company of Hope. They had been thick as thieves together in high school and she trusted that their relationship had not changed. She was a bit apprehensive about what Hope would think of her marriage to Kurt, knowing how opinionated her friend could be. Kurt's sister was okay, and her little girl was as sweet as pie. As for the rest of the people on the guest list, she hardly knew any of them and would be perfectly happy if it stayed that way.

Kurt walked over to his own closet to change clothes and thought, I can't wait to show off my new bride and island mansion to the guests. The conversion of the place had ended up being a success beyond his expectations. Turning the hotel, which had operated at a loss, into his own private getaway was a stroke of genius.

The formal invitations went out in February and were met with mixed feelings among the recipients. They read:

"You are cordially invited to Kurt and Barbie's wedding celebration. The official wedding, which took place last month, was a private ceremony with only family and close friends. As the conversion of my hotel on the Isle of Ease into a vacation residence will be completed this spring, we would like to share the spot with you. It will be a week-long party, taking place from April 8 to April 14.

Here are the particulars: I will arrange for you to board a commercial return-flight to Honolulu, Hawaii, scheduled to get there before 2:00 p.m. on Saturday, April 8. A charter boat will take you to the island on that afternoon and will return you to Honolulu at the end of the week, Friday, April 14. During your stay, you can enjoy snorkeling, scuba diving, deep-sea fishing, or just relax on the beach and around the pool. We also have some indoor activities that may be of interest.

Please RSVP by March 5."

It was signed:

"Looking forward to celebrate with you,
Kurt and Barbie Nobel"

There was a list of requested guests attached, which read:

"Kim Frederique with Evie Frederique
Hope De Luca
Neal Victor
Alexa and Max Weller
Sidney and Heather Ross
Rafi and Kate Simonian
Mike and Beatrice Triest."

CHAPTER 2

Prosperous Max Weller, who made his fortune in generic drugs and medical patents, read the invitation twice and thought, weird, but interesting. He did not even attempt to guess how his wife, Alexa, would react. After four years together he should have been able to read her, but she remained a puzzle to him. Their marriage was on shaky grounds as of late, which made things even more complicated. He mulled over their issues, then shook off the eerie feeling that suddenly struck him and went online to do a bit of research.

Meanwhile, Alexa Weller was stuck on the 134 Freeway, homebound from her Westside law office to their home in South Pasadena. Even at 7:30 in the evening, traffic was still heavy. The 37-year-old defense attorney was a brunette with striking light-blue eyes that contrasted with her dark-brown hair. She was of medium height and slender, but her practice of wearing three-inch heals during trials made her look tall and imposing. Like all successful trial lawyers, she had a way with words and a knack for convincing people of her point of view. Her most compelling attribute to her professional triumphs was her low, commanding voice. Jurors had no choice but to take notice.

On that end-of-day commute, Alexa's mind was first in work-mode, dwelling on her current case, but when the traffic jam eased and she got closer to South Pasadena, her thoughts drifted to what awaited her at home. What had gone wrong in her marriage? she wondered. Even before her little unimportant fling, things had no longer been harmonious between her and Max. They hardly talked to one another, each absorbed with their career. And when they did spend time together, they treaded on egg shells, careful not to broach the subject that was at the core of their dispute. He wanted children, and she definitely did not. She had made it clear before tying the knot that she neither had time nor patience to raise kids. Max, seven years her senior, seemed to have forgotten about that agreement and was now pressuring her into changing her mind.

To her surprise, she found Max waiting for her in the foyer when she got home.

He asked, "Have you had dinner?"

"No, I'm starved."

"Maria prepared a chicken dish before she left. I ate mine and you may reheat yours in the microwave."

Alexa thought, our housekeeper is a gem. Aloud she said sardonically, "Is there a reason you're greeting me at the door?"

"I'll tell you after you've eaten."

He followed her into the kitchen, waited until she was done with her meal, then sat down on a stool next to hers at the center aisle. He handed her the Nobels' invitation, saying, "This came with today's mail."

She read the sheet of paper, then laughed out loud.

"You find this amusing?"

"Highly! It is typical of the egomaniac to exhibit his singer trophy wife on his vacation paradise."

"His bride is a singer?"

"You must have heard of her; she's called 'Barbie.'"

"I may have, but I don't pay attention to pop music."

She asked, "Where is this Isle of Ease? I'm aware that Kurt owned a hotel on some island, but was never curious as to its location."

Max said, "I did some research before you got home. Isle of Ease is a tiny island, approximately 30 nautical miles southwest of the Hawaiian Islands. In fact, Kurt Nobel owns the entire island. It is too small to be drawn on any map and belongs to the jurisdiction of the US. The place is totally isolated with no population to speak of. The hotel was basically the only thing on it; no wonder it wasn't a success. The spot may be a tropical paradise, but who wants to be excluded from civilization in our day and age? Also, I can imagine that all supplies had to be hauled by boat or helicopter, which could hardly contribute to a profitable venture."

Then he said, "Did you read the guest list?"

"Oh, is there a second page?" She reached for it, then chuckled again as she read it.

"Do you know any of these people personally?"

She nodded, "Some, and others I've heard of. Kim is Kurt's sister and Evie is her daughter. Evie must be around eight by now. We know who Neal Victor is, of course."

Max put in, "Yep. He's our congressman and Kurt Nobel ran against him and lost, making it one of the rare occasions in politics when integrity won over money."

"Exactly. They were opponents and ran a nasty campaign with Neal Victor being the *victor*. How hilarious!"

Alexa continued with her finger on the guest list, "Sidney Ross is Kurt's CFO, and the names Mike and

Beatrice Triest sound familiar, but I can't place them at the moment. I don't know who Hope De Luca is, nor have I heard of Rafi or Kate Simonian."

He said, "I googled these people and your recollection is correct. Heather, the wife of Sidney Ross, is a librarian. As for the Simonians, Rafi is listed as entrepreneur and his spouse, Kate, writes mystery novels. Mike Triest and Kurt are colleagues in real estate development. I take that back, colleagues is not the right term; they are rivals. Triest's wife is a homemaker who volunteers at high-end charitable events. I could not find any information on Hope De Luca."

Neither spoke for several seconds. Max finally said, "You never told me the reason you broke up with Kurt only days before the wedding."

"I got cold feet," she replied, "but my main issue was that he tried to run me."

"I see. Nobody could ever "run you" and that's a fact."

Alexa tagged him with an intense stare, checking for sarcasm, but his features remained expressionless.

He asked, "Why do you think he invited us?"

"That's easy. He wants to show me, and everyone else on his crazy guest list, his dish of a wife, while at the same time flaunting his exotic island."

There was another pause. Then Max probed, "Do you feel the urge to spend a week with a bunch of unconnected people who may or may not hate their host's guts?"

She took her time before she answered, "My first impulse was to decline the invitation. No way was I going to obey his summons and take part in his childish power game. On second thought, though, I'm curious. The weird trip might turn into a satisfying adventure."

She checked her calendar on the smart phone and mumbled, "April 8 to April 14 is the week before Easter.

My current case goes to trial on March 7 and will last no more than three weeks. I was thinking of taking some time off after it is over to go somewhere to relax." She grinned and added, "This would be a paid vacation."

For the first time since their conversation started, a slight smile appeared on Max's face, making him look younger and less grim. A brief realization crossed Alexa's mind. This is the face I fell in love with: dark, handsome, and kind.

He said, "A relaxing trip to a peaceful, exotic island may even salvage our marriage."

"We'll see. I'm making no promises," she replied.

"So, are we going?"

"Yes, let's find out what millionaire Kurt and his teenage bride have planned for their guests."

"Is she really still in her teens?"

"I don't know, but she looks it. He should have no trouble 'running' her."

Max got up and was already at the kitchen door when Alexa called, "I have a condition about the outlandish trip, though."

As he turned to face her, she stated in her low, commanding voice, "There will be no mention of my little fling, nor any discussion about having kids."

"Understood," he agreed.

CHAPTER 3

Kim Frederique, middle school English teacher and single mom, sat in the family room of her condominium in Arcadia, a stack of ungraded students' papers in front of her. She was 44, with light-brown hair, green eyes, and an athletic body. Evie, her little girl, had long been tucked in bed, following her evening bedtime story. Kim was trying to get through the heap of students' compositions but could not concentrate. Her mind crept back to the bizarre invitation she had received in the mail that day. Hers came with an extra note inserted, which read:

"Hi Sis,

Since you were unable to attend our wedding, I trust you'll enjoy the party on the Isle of Ease. You may not know most of the guests, but take my word for it, they are an interesting and fun group of people. I am sorry that Evie will be the only child present, but some of the activities - - like snorkeling and swimming - - should keep her from getting bored.

"Can't wait to celebrate with you,

Kurt"

It was true that she had been sick in the hospital with pneumonia when her brother's wedding took place, but this "after the fact" celebration seemed totally uncalled for. As far as she knew, Kurt had taken Barbie on an elaborate honeymoon to Australia. Why can't he give it a rest now? she mused. Of course, he needs to show off the mansion on his island. She had never been there when it was a hotel and was not particularly keen on going there now. She doubted that wearing bathing suits among women with perfect bodies like Barbie and Alexa would boost her self-image.

For another thing, even though she loved him, being around her older brother made her feel like a poor relation. Granted, he had always been generous, but she hated to feel like a charity case. Evie adored her uncle Kurt, who tended to spoil her. Would it matter to Evie if she had no kids to play with for a week? Being an only child, she was able to entertain herself. And she enjoyed swimming and water games. Kim was certain that her daughter would be thrilled to go on the trip. The timing was also right. April 8 – 14 was during spring break.

She studied the guest list once more. Why on earth was he inviting Alexa? He must really want to rub it in by showing off the young, talented, and seemingly flawless Barbie. Reflecting on Kurt's choice of women, his first wife had definitely been best suited to him. Too bad the marriage did not last. But then, who am I to judge? I'm also divorced. He has two fine boys resulting from that union. She corrected herself; they are young adults now.

Then came arrogant Alexa with whom he had had a love/hate relationship. In Kim's opinion, Alexa had an ego to match her brother's. The woman's only vulnerability was her asthma, and she even used that to her own advantage. Kurt had been obsessed with her and had taken it hard when she broke off the engagement. Who could blame him for feeling humiliated? After the breakup and until Barbie, he did casual dating, but nothing serious. Kim was not sure about Barbie. Other than being too young for Kurt, who was into his fifth decade, she had nothing against the singer. She assumed that her brother had been wise enough to insist on a pre-nuptial agreement.

The craziest choice of guest by far was Neal Victor. What strange demon possessed Kurt to invite that member of the House of Representatives? As far as she could tell, the two men hated one another. The supposedly idyllic festivity on the isle could well turn into a hostile environment of hidden power players.

Oh, what the heck, she mused, I don't have enough drama in my life. Might as well accept the invitation. The decision made, she at last turned her attention to the stack of papers awaiting her.

Twenty-five miles farther west at his home in North Hollywood, Neal Victor stared at the invitation. The recently widowed congressman wondered if this was a joke. He re-read it once more and decided that Kurt Nobel must be suffering from delusions of grandeur. At first, the idea of partying with his onetime enemy seemed out of the question, but reading the guest list made him reconsider. One person on that list caught his attention.

He didn't really want to meet the young bride, imagining that she would be a looker and ambitious, like most gold diggers. But exploring the small island, scuba diving in particular, captured his interest. Getting away would be a welcome distraction after months of grieving. But why is Nobel inviting me to this event? he asked himself. Is he considering running for office again and in need of political favors? If so, he can shove it, paid trip or not. Or maybe he needs a tax write-off. It certainly couldn't be out of pure kindness.

To hell with second-guessing the man's ulterior motive. There's nothing wrong with accepting a free vacation. Contrary to public opinion, members of congress' salaries were not high, given the need to maintain two households, one in their home state and another in Washington, DC.

His mind was made up. He would put his RSVP in the next day's mail.

Barbie's best friend from high school, Hope De Luca, was thrilled to receive the invitation. As a sophomore in college on the East Coast, the young woman had missed out on her friend's wedding. She had come from a family of meager means and attended the University on a full scholarship. Taking time out for the wedding had not been an option. Fortunately, the week of this celebration would coincide with her spring break, and she was enthusiastic to be among the guests. The entire trip was going to be paid for; she did not have to spend a dime. How cool was that!

Hope was curious about Kurt Nobel too, having never met the man. She understood he was a rich, real estate tycoon. Other than that, she knew nothing about him. Apparently, Barbie had known Kurt less than a year and, in Hope's opinion, had rushed into the marriage. The young woman could not imagine what he had in common with Barbie but hoped to find out in April. She and Barbie were opposites in looks as well as aptitudes. Her friend was a fair beauty and she herself was dark-haired with big brown eyes. Barbie was musically inclined and had skipped college, whereas Hope could not carry a tune but had a logical, scientific mind.

She looked out her dorm window to a harsh landscape of snow and ice. Judging by the dark clouds above, more of the white stuff would be dumped before the day was over. Hope shivered and could hardly wait for the warm, tropical days in the sun that lay ahead.

CHAPTER 4

The Triests, both middle aged, were not in agreement about whether or not to accept the invitation.

Mike insisted, "Come on, Beatrice, aren't you the least bit curious about Kurt's palace on the Isle of Ease? I'm interested to see what he's done to the place."

She shook her head.

He tried to convince her from a different angle and coaxed, "At the beginning of April, you'll be tired from organizing the fundraiser fashion show and more than ready to relax on a tropical island."

"Have you read the guest list?" she asked.

"Of course I have and know what's on your mind. I'm not thrilled about it either."

She shot him an angry glance and burst out, "There is no way in hell that I'll socialize with the likes of Alexa Weller."

"Neither will I, but there'll be plenty of other folks to mingle with. We can ignore the attorney."

"You may be able to ignore her, but I can't. She'll be a constant reminder of the injustice done to us."

Mike stated with conviction, "I can almost guarantee you that we won't come face to face with her. Most likely, Alexa will decline the invitation."

"You think?"

"She dumped Kurt at the last moment, remember? I can't see why he invited her, and even less why she would show up."

"You may be right."

"I bet you I'm right," her spouse said.

Beatrice said, "And while we're on the subject, why did he invite us? You're not exactly best friends."

"That's a no-brainer. He wants to rub my nose in all he has accomplished on his island."

"That's not bothering you?"

"On the contrary. I'm nosy and looking forward to it."

"Unwinding on an exotic island would be peaceful," she admitted.

"So let's go."

"Okay," she said, hoping that she would not regret her decision.

The conversation taking place at the Ross residence had a different tone.

Sidney, Kurt Nobel's CFO, was in his fifties with grown children. His round, jolly face lit up as he remarked, "This is better than the actual wedding. I'm flattered that he chose us to be among his guests, and I'm interested to see what he's done with that monster of a hotel on the island."

Heather was petite, keeping her slight figure even during menopause. She said, "I didn't know that you ever saw the place when it was a hotel."

"I never did, but the resort was such a money guzzler, operating in the red, that I suggested he should get rid of it. It was Kurt's own idea to turn it into his private vacation residence, which makes sense, since it would have been nearly impossible to sell."

She laughed and remarked, "I'm surprised your millionaire boss is going to the trouble of arranging flights for everybody on a commercial airliner to Hawaii and a boat trip from there to the location. I would have thought he'd use his private jet to get us there directly."

Sidney said, "That's not an option. There is no runway on the island. It is only accessible by boat or helicopter."

"Of course. How stupid of me!" Then she said, "I have some vacation time due. Tomorrow, I'll let them know at the library about taking that week in April off." She nudged her husband playfully and said, "It will be a wonderful, unexpected trip. I'm already excited!"

The Simonian family had finished their dinner. The boys, one a senior in high school, the other a sophomore, had carried their plates to the dishwasher and then vanished into their bedrooms to do homework, listen to music, and text their friends. Kate ran coffees through the espresso machine, then carried the small cups - - one for Rafi, the other for her - - to the dining room.

Their relationship had not lost its spark after twenty-four years of marriage. Kate admired her spouse for his ingenuity in business and sensitivity in matters of the heart. For his part, he appreciated her quick mind and ability to keep their family as a welcoming unit, despite everyone's busy lives. The fact that she was still a good-looking woman was a bonus.

Between sips, she said, "That's quite a surprise we got in the mail today."

"No kidding!"

"Do you have time to go on the trip?"

"I'll make time. This is too good to miss," Rafi assured her.

"What about our sons?"

"The boys are mature and trustworthy enough to fend for themselves for a week," Rafi said with confidence.

"I guess so."

He winked and said, "Imagine what a leisurely vacation on a tropical island can do for our love life, not to mention all the ideas the romantic setting will provide for your next book."

"Your enthusiasm is contagious on both accounts! I had better get myself in gear, then."

"What do you mean?"

"Purchase an exotic summer wardrobe," she replied.

CHAPTER 5

At the beginning of March was a rare occasion when Kurt and Barbie dined together at home, just the two of them. The domestics had their day off and Barbie cooked the meal herself, which was also a rarity. She'd done her own grocery shopping, followed by a couple hours of labor in the kitchen. She now served them meatloaf, mashed potatoes and gravy, and green beans.

Kurt took a few bites and then praised, "Nothing compares to a wholesome, home-cooked meal. You're not only gorgeous but an excellent cook as well!"

Clearly pleased, Barbie did not let on that she was a novice, having followed the cookbook's recipes, step by step.

As they lingered over coffee, Kurt announced, "We got the last response in today's mail. Now all have replied and are planning to attend our celebration."

I was afraid of that, Barbie thought, but kept it to herself.

He continued, "I'll go ahead and book the flights and arrange for the boat ride. I'll also organize the domestic aspect of our venture. You don't need to do anything as far as that goes, but I'm asking a favor." Grinning, he said, "You can probably guess what that is."

She gave him a blank stare.

"I'd like you to sing for our guests."

She shook her head. "I'd rather not."

"You love to perform. So what's the problem?"

"I don't feel secure singing without accompaniment."

"Of course you'll have backup music. For one thing, there's already a grand piano at our place on the Isle of Ease and - -"

"There is?" she interrupted.

"How could I plan a vacation house without a piano for you to play on? But don't worry. I don't expect you to sing and play at the same time for the guests. I can engage musicians. How about the band you used to belong to? We'll hire them if they're available."

She grimaced and said, "They're angry at me for having quit, leaving them without a lead singer. They're a proud bunch; I doubt they'd come."

"Doesn't matter. I'll find you other backup musicians. Meanwhile, you can all practice here in your music room."

He did not give her a chance for objections and said, "That's settled then. Leave it all to me."

Later, deep into the night, while Kurt was snoring next to her, Barbie lay awake. She wondered, are all millionaires like that? She had not been permitted to make a single decision of her own, ever since their wedding day. On closer reflection, the controlling had started even before, without her having been aware of it. Well, she determined, I'll get back at him in my own way. Tomorrow, I'll call for the chauffeur and have him drop me off at Rodeo Drive for some serious shopping.

CHAPTER 6

Domenica Cortes had been Kurt Nobel's live-in housekeeper at his Beverly Hills estate for many years, ever since the divorce from his first wife. She was a widow with two grown daughters, one living in nearby Culver City with husband and elementary school age kids, the other in Guadalajara, Mexico, with a no-good-husband and two teenagers.

At the moment, Domenica was laundering the master bedroom sheets. Fortunately, the task did not require her full attention, as her mind was stuck on the conversation she'd had that morning with Señor Nobel. He had asked her to be in charge of the household on his little island while he entertained guests there. She had come up with all sorts of excuses why she could not go there in April, and he had managed to overturn them all.

Assuming that she worried the job was too much work for one person, he had assured her that he didn't expect her to take care of the domestic needs of him, his new wife, and a dozen guests all on her own. He would leave it up to her to hire more help as she thought fit. Señor Nobel had it all wrong, none of that had entered her mind. She was too embarrassed to let him know that the reason she was reluctant to do the job was her fear of flying. In all of her sixty years, she had avoided traveling by air, and hoped to keep it that way. Her motto was, *if God intended us to fly, we would have wings.*

While switching sheets from washer to dryer, Domenica thought, so why did I end up agreeing to his offer? Money, of course. Señor Nobel will pay me double the salary for that week in April and an extra-large bonus, for what he called "my trouble." True, her employer was, and always had been, generous. Since having few expenses - - being a live-in, her board and food was taken care of - - she was able to put a large part of her earnings in the bank. In another two years, she should have enough saved to retire and buy a nice house in a good neighborhood of Guadalajara. Her plan was to share that house with her older daughter, who could then afford to get rid of that savage husband of hers.

Domenica tried not to dwell on the scary five-hour flight that awaited her. Instead, she concentrated on the practical side of the undertaking. She recalled the end of her talk with Señor Nobel. He had said, "It is your decision who and how many helpers you want to take along. I trust your judgement. The only requirement is that they are legally documented in the US. I will pay them more than the going rate for domestics, and of course take care of their travel expenses. I haven't yet talked to Hermina Tovar, our cook, but see no reason why she'd refuse to come on board." To that, she had answered, "With Hermina in charge of the kitchen, I'll only need one person to help me. Between the two of us, we can cope with a dozen people." Then Señor Nobel had asked if she had someone in mind, which she did. And now she needed to ask that person and then report back to him.

Domenica's choice was her friend Rosa, a homemaker who would welcome earning some extra money. She was sure her friend was going to jump at the chance but uncertain whether her husband, Carlos, would let her go. He was old-fashioned regarding his wife. If Rosa couldn't come, she had at least three other people in mind who would be more than happy to fill the spot.

My daughters won't believe me when I'll tell them that I'm flying to Honolulu, Hawaii, she thought. In fact, she had a hard time believing it herself.

CHAPTER 7

Kurt, Barbie, and their domestic employees were on the way to the island a day ahead of time to get the place ready. On Friday, April 7, they boarded an early-morning flight from LAX to Honolulu, Hawaii. Except for a few executives, the newlyweds and the musicians hired for Barbie's performance had the business class cabin to themselves. Kurt had booked a couple of extra seats to accommodate the band's instruments.

Soon after takeoff, Kurt reached for Barbie's hand and said, "You'll love the Isle of Ease! This coming week is dedicated to celebrating with our friends, but afterwards, we can vacation on it anytime we please."

She nodded, but was doubtful whether she would have the time of her life there. From what she'd gathered, the place was cut off from civilization, not exactly a happening spot.

She asked, "How big is it, again?"

"The isle is less than 0.4 square miles. It doesn't even take an hour to walk its perimeter."

"And there are no other people on it?"

"Our estate is at the southern shore with no one nearby. On the north shore, I've rented out a few vacation cabins, and an old Polynesian hermit lives on that part of the island. He wasn't happy when I built the hotel. I have no idea how he feels about the private residence. There is also a general store up there, but it's not always in operation."

"So how does the hermit get his supplies when the store is closed?"

"As far as I know, a boat with provisions, such as food and other necessities, anchors periodically at the north shore. Maybe monthly, or once every two weeks. I'm not sure." He smiled at her and said, "You won't come in contact with the man, so don't worry about him."

Back in economy class, Domenica kept her eyes closed in silent prayer. At take-off, when the jet engine had made the most horrible racket and she had been pushed deep into her seat during the steep ascent, it had taken all her self-control not to scream out loud in panic. Instead, she had held on tight to Hermina to her left and Rosa on her right. Her grip had been hard and would likely leave blue marks on both their arms.

Now, with the seatbelt sign off and the plane cruising steadily above the clouds, Domenica made the sign of the cross, thanking God to have survived so far. And when the flight attendant offered her a snack, she gratefully accepted it, realizing that she was starved. She had skipped breakfast at home, too nervous to eat with the worry of the ordeal that lay ahead.

The two men in the seats immediately behind Domenica and Rosa introduced themselves - - not bothering with last names - - after realizing they were both part of the Nobel household.

"I'm Chris, the pool maintenance guy," the young, sun-bleached towhead said, "and I've seen you around the Beverly Hills Estate. You're the gardener, right?"

The middle-aged Latino said, "My name is Emilio and I think for the next week I'll be more like the maintenance person. There isn't much gardening to be done. For instance, I have to install strings of lights and set up tables and chairs in preparation for the outdoor party tomorrow night. And for the rest of the week, I need to make sure the grounds surrounding the vacation house are in tip-top shape. Should be a piece of cake. Mr. Nobel assured me that all equipment needed is still there from when the place was a hotel." He chuckled and added, "I'm also gonna be the official porter, helping people with their luggage."

"I was told to give you a hand when needed, as taking care of the pool won't keep me busy for long."

"Good to know."

Chris asked, "What is the name of the boat we are to board out of Honolulu?"

"I don't remember. The boss flies on the same plane. Knowing him, he'll have an escort show us the way to the harbor and his yacht if he can't do it himself."

"Have you been to the Hawaiian islands before?"

Emilio replied, "My wife bought a church raffle ticket and won a trip for two to Maui a few years ago. We loved the place. I haven't been on Oahu or any of the other islands."

"I've never visited there at all. Come to think of it, I've never even been farther south than the Baja California Peninsula." Seconds later he wanted to know, "Do you suppose we'll have time to visit Pearl Harbor?"

"No way, young man! We're not tourists but the working crew. Remember?"

That established, they donned their headsets, and Emilio watched a movie while Chris played video games.

CHAPTER 8

Kurt had it all arranged like clockwork. Bedding, linens, and other nonperishable supplies had been transported to the island previously. On that Friday, a day ahead of the guests, they lunched on sandwiches on his yacht before he moored it at the Isle of Ease's landing. He told Barbie to wait while he escorted the domestics and musicians to their accommodations in a separate structure behind the main house, which had served as the hotel employees' quarters.

When he came back with the gardener, who would help with their luggage, he found Barbie at shore's edge, looking up at the three-story dwelling, mesmerized.

Kurt said, "You like the looks of it?"

Entranced, she replied, "It's an enchanted castle!"

He nodded. "I opted for a fairytale appearance with the hotel's exterior. As for the remodeling, I had them change the overall look as little as possible. Most of the conversion was done to the interior."

As they approached the entrance, he made a point of carrying her over the threshold, ignoring the weak spot in his back that periodically flared up.

From the outside, the building gave the impression of a charmed castle out of a fabled storybook, but once one stepped indoors, the place was modern with every contemporary comfort imaginable. From the high ceiling entrance hall, there was a spiral staircase leading up to the second and third floors, but Kurt led them straight to the elevator.

Stepping into it and pushing "P" for penthouse, he turned to Barbie and said, "I'll show you around the ground floor later. I'm sure you're anxious to unpack and freshen up."

When entering the master bedrooms he thanked the gardener, now acting porter, for his help and dismissed him.

Barbie checked out the gigantic rooms. The first sported a sturdy four-post king-size traditional style mahogany bed with matching dresser, armoire, and nightstands. A big-screen TV took up most of the space on the wall, and the walk-in closet was a room on its own. She sauntered through all of it and the connecting sitting room, hardly giving the massive spaces any attention. Then she stepped into the second bedroom, and a sound of pure pleasure escaped her as she looked the place over.

The French country décor was spot on to her liking. The champagne and ivory queen-size bed, made from birch wood, was flanked by a matching nightstand and dresser. The mirror above the chest of drawers was accented with Swarovski crystals. Barbie went over to the bed and examined the luxurious pillow-tufted headboard and then ran a finger along its equally crafted footboard. She did not bother to look inside her walk-in closet, knowing that it would be spacious and practical, but turned to Kurt who had followed her into the room.

"It's perfect," she exclaimed. "How did you know my taste in furniture?"

"I'll keep that my little secret," he replied with a smirk. In reality, he had taken a guess. Knowing that she liked feminine things, he had asked the interior designer for recommendations. French country was one of the styles suggested.

Both bedrooms led to adjacent bathrooms with marble tubs equipped with Jacuzzi jets. Barbie gave hers a casual glance and then stepped back into the bedroom and went over to the vast sliding glass door which led to the balcony. Kurt unfastened and slid it open and they both stepped out onto the terrace. The view down to the mansion's garden and pool area to one side, the tropical, wild island vegetation to the other, and the wide ocean beyond took Barbie's breath away.

"Everything looks magical from up here," she exclaimed.

"No arguing with that," he said.

"From the landing, as I first looked up at the castle, I noticed that there's one continuous balcony wrapped around the entire second floor."

"You are observant! As a hotel, each room had its individual balcony. When I had the builders remodel most of the second story into guest bedrooms, they got rid of some walls, making the rooms larger and connecting the balconies into one giant terrace. There is access to it from every room now. The interior designers allotted each guestroom its own theme, making the place look like a residence and no longer a resort."

He reached for her hand and said, "Let me show you the rest of the third floor, and then I'll leave you alone, so that you can get settled."

They went on a tour of the gym, which contained standard workout equipment: treadmills, stationary bicycles, rowers, and climbers. There was also a huge room with a practice putting green made of artificial grass. Kurt pointed out that although there was no golf course on the island, he could at least perfect his putting skills. And low and behold, the last room was an office with a desk and chair, computer, printer, shredder, and a bookcase stacked with professional books pertaining to real estate development.

Surprised, Barbie asked, "Are you planning to work here?"

"Not this week, but yes, on future trips."

They were walking back to their bedrooms when the peaceful quiet of the island was interrupted. She turned his way and cried out, "What's that horrible noise?"

"That's the helicopter transporting food and drink supplies. I bet Hermina is relieved to hear its sound. She worried that the pantry in her kitchen would stay empty. By the way, the chopper will return to the isle on Sunday morning to fly the musicians back to Honolulu." He added, "Sounds like he's about ready to touch ground. I need to go down and direct traffic."

Unpacking did not take Barbie long, and as she soaked in her luxurious marble tub, she thought, I could learn to like this place. The rest of her day was pretty much taken up with rehearsals for the performance she was to give the next evening. The musicians had the hard job of organizing the stage. Emilio helped them move the grand piano, but the rest was up to the band. They were in charge of setting up the audio equipment by linking the guitar cables to the amplifier; testing the microphones and perfecting the acoustics for the outdoor show; tuning their instruments; and last but most importantly, practicing the pieces of music Barbie had chosen. All *she* had to do was sing.

CHAPTER 9

The charter boat dropped the guests off in the late afternoon on Saturday. Approaching the mansion, their remarks ranged from "How lovely" to "It's a pretentious castle!"

They were shown to their respective guest bedrooms on the second floor to unpack and freshen up. Then followed a tour given by their host who guided them through the ground floor. There was a state-of-the-art kitchen and bar, large living and dining rooms, den with a TV screen extending over an entire wall, a music room, a couple of bathrooms, and his pride and joy, the game room.

As he walked them through the game room, he stated, "Feel free to compete in a game of pool, ping pong, or foosball. And for those of you with arcade video nostalgia, enjoy the vintage Ms Pacman, Donkey Kong, and pinball machines." On the third floor, he mentioned that the workout equipment in the gym and the practice putting green were at their disposal.

In the early evening, people gathered for the after-wedding-celebration in the mansion's garden. Folding tables and chairs were set up in a semi-circle around a temporary stage. Strings of lights hung from several fragrant mimosa trees, wrapping their yellow flowers in a deep golden sheen. Additional light from the tabletop lanterns added to the romantic atmosphere as dusk turned into night.

Set off to the side, Hermina roasted prime rib on a giant barbecue grill. Chris tended the bar, mixing exotic cocktails like Mai Tais, daiquiris, piña coladas, and margaritas. No dress code applied. Kurt's specification "island party casual" left people to their own interpretation. Most men showed up in Hawaiian shirts and either shorts or khakis. Whereas the women had chosen flowery dresses or wraparound skirts.

Alexa was one of the exceptions. Flower design clothing cramped her style. Happy to leave her tailored suits at home, she dazzled in an azure-blue backless dress. The invitees, glasses filled with fruity drinks, stood around in small groups chatting, and then ambled toward the set tables.

Neal found space at a table where Kim and her little girl were seated next to Hope. Sidney and Heather Ross had already socialized with the Triests on the boat ride over, so it was only natural that the four would dine together. Each setting accommodated four or five people, except one small table for two near the stage, which everyone presumed was reserved for the newlyweds. After Max and Alexa collected their margaritas, the only available seats were next to the Simonians. Alexa and Max introduced themselves.

Rafi thought, she doesn't remember me, but I clearly recall the day I ran into Kurt and his then fiancée. At the time I supposed that the man was not thinking straight, otherwise he'd have stuck with the wife who was a good woman in Rafi's estimation, and not hook up with Alexa. But he had to admit, Alexa was still as attractive now as she had been then, but her high-brow demeanor was even more pronounced. All this went through Rafi's mind in seconds, and he decided to keep their previous encounter to himself.

He formally said, "Pleased to meet you both. We are Rafi and Kate Simonian."

Alexa asked - - less out of curiosity but feeling the need to make small talk - - "How do you folks know Kurt and Barbie?"

Rafi replied, "Kurt and I go back a long way. Our older son and his youngest played on the same neighborhood soccer team as little boys. Kurt and I hit it off and stayed friends all these years."

Alexa's trial attorney's skill for noticing detail was evident as she said, "So you live in Beverly Hills?"

Rafi smiled and said, "In those days, Kurt and his family lived in Glendale." He touched Kate's hand in a gentle gesture and remarked, "We still live there in our same house."

Max was not paying attention to their conversation but eyed his wife while mulling over his own agenda. He thought, Alexa may think of her infidelity as an insignificant, spur-of-the-moment fling, but no matter how brief, she committed adultery and betrayed me. He was determined to keep his word to not bring up the subject yet doubted that he could ever let it go in his mind or come to terms with it.

Suddenly aware that both Simonians were looking at him, expecting his contribution to their topic, Max was about to add an incidental remark. He didn't get the chance, however, because their hosts made an impressive entrance onto the garden scene. A spotlight, controlled by Emilio from the mansion's balcony, followed the pair as they walked hand in hand past their guests and onto the stage. Barbie stunned in an off-white, sleeveless charmeuse dress. Kurt wore off-white trousers and a silk shirt, which matched the purple tropical flower in his bride's hair.

Domenica and Rosa went from table to table, pouring champagne into people's glasses, except for Evie's, who received Hawaiian punch instead.

"Welcome to the Isle of Ease," Kurt started his speech. "I'm glad you've all come to join Barbie and me in celebrating our new lives together, and hope that you'll enjoy your stay. It will be a week of good food and sea adventures, but most important, one of relaxation and peace among friends. If we had our differences in the past, I want to take this opportunity to show that there are no hard feelings."

He looked straight at Alexa when uttering that last sentence, and she had a hard time keeping from bursting out laughing.

He continued, "I want each and every one of you to have a good time, so let me know of any special wishes to make your experience here more comfortable. If you have a craving for a snack or drink between meals, our cook, Hermina, will be happy to accommodate you. My housekeeper, Domenica, and her helper Rosa are in charge of domestic issues. If you need anything done to your room or if your clothing needs laundering, either one of those ladies can help you."

He grinned at Mike Triest, "No real estate talk, please." Pointing a finger at Neal Victor, he ordered, "And most essential, no political talk!"

"Fine by me," the latter shot back.

Kurt motioned to Chris at the bar, who took his cue and hurried over to hand each newlywed a glass of champagne.

Their host raised his glass, and as all guests did likewise, he proposed a toast, "To my lovely Barbie! May we live happily ever after. To you, my baby sister, favorite niece, and friends, have an amazing week!"

"Hear, hear!" some of the guests cheered.

Hope had inwardly cringed during the entire lecture. How could Barbie have married such a pompous ass? And he was ancient too! She had thought that she knew her friend inside out, but apparently that was not the case. If only she'd been around Barbie before the wedding, she'd have talked some sense into her. So what if the guy is loaded? Money isn't that important, at least not in my book, Hope thought.

Minutes later, the party was in full swing. The prime rib with all its trimmings tasted excellent, and the drinks helped everyone relax. While dessert of tiramisu, coffee and tea was being served, Kurt announced that Barbie had a special treat planned. She and her musicians filed onto the stage, which was promptly spotlighted.

Barbie sang a total of four pieces of music. She had chosen carefully among her repertoire of songs, keeping some of her middle-aged audience in mind - - nothing too racy, she had reminded herself. Her performance included two popular numbers from her latest album, a ballad, and a moving gospel tune to end the concert.

The spectators were mesmerized throughout her show. The young woman had a strong, rich voice with a wide range. She was not only an excellent singer but an outstanding performer, knowing how to captivate and engage her audience.

Between numbers, Sidney Ross shouted with enthusiasm, "Wow, the girl can *sing!*"

Hope, who had heard her friend sing in high school musicals and as the lead singer of a band, was blown away. Barbie had been blessed with a good voice to begin with, but she'd perfected her role as a performer. The way she worked the microphone was worth taking notice, let alone the way she moved around the stage. Ending with the revered gospel song was pure genius and touched each guest deeply. Beatrice Triest was moved to tears.

The applause, shouts of "bravo," and standing ovation gave Barbie a rush. No matter the size of her audience, whether a crowd of hundreds or only a dozen, the gratification remained the same.

CHAPTER 10

Sunday morning after breakfast, as the helicopter noise carrying the musicians faded away in the distance, Kurt announced, "There is no church on the island, but you can worship in God's underwater universe. Besides deep-sea fishing gear, I also keep snorkeling and scuba diving equipment in the shed close to the shore. Of course, diving is only for those of you with scuba certification. You can either go on a dive from land, or I'll take you out on the yacht."

The Triests, regular church goers, did not see the humor in his joke about worshiping underwater. Mike sent a reassuring glance toward his wife, meaning, *don't take offense.*

Soon the guests took part in their chosen activities. The divers walked over to the shed at the water's edge to get their scuba tanks filled, via an air compressor, and equipped themselves with scuba gear. They used the buddy system for the dives. Kim paired up with Neal, and Kurt with Rafi. Kurt kept a variety of wetsuits in the shed, but all four came prepared and had brought their own. For now, they decided to do shore diving. Later in the week, they would venture out by boat.

Kurt and Rafi took the lead, with Kurt showing them the way. They walked right over the volcanic rock, then swam the short distance out to the reef on the surface before descending down to it. And so the underwater exploring began. Each person stayed close to his or her buddy for safety reasons. Should something go wrong with the equipment, there would be the other diver to help out. The pairs used sign language to point out fish, underwater creatures, and coral formations. For the next hour, all four divers tuned out the world above and gave their full attention to the colorful wonders of the sea.

Sidney and Heather Ross, Kate Simonian, and Max Weller opted to go snorkeling. Alexa had planned to try snorkeling too but chickened out as soon as she saw the snorkels and masks.

"Worried about the asthma?" Max asked.

She nodded and said, "Better be safe than sorry. I'll go swimming and relax around the pool instead."

Kim had promised to take Evie snorkeling in the afternoon. In the meantime, the Triests offered to watch the child while she swam in the pool.

Emilio and Chris were busy taking the temporary stage apart. They had rolled the piano back to the music room and returned the folding tables and chairs to storage already the night before. Seeing the people about to dive and snorkel walking past them toward the ocean, Chris said, "I wish I could go snorkeling too."

Annoyed, Emilio told him, "We are here to work and get paid well for it, so shut up and do your job." And without missing a beat he pointed out, "I saw a couple of hammocks in storage. Let's hang them between the palm trees close to the landing."

Chris thought, the man is a work machine. I got up at the crack of dawn to take care of the pool and was barely done adding chemicals and hosing down the deck, when he ordered me to come help with taking the stage down. What's the hurry? I'm sure it could have waited until tomorrow. And now he has already stuff planned for when we're done here.

As if Emilio could read his mind, he remarked, "Once we've set up the hammocks, you can relax in one of them, it being Sunday and all."

CHAPTER 11

Barbie was not a water rat; she could swim, but underwater activities like snorkeling made her feel claustrophobic. Hope had acted strangely toward her on the night before and also that morning at breakfast.

Barbie turned to her and said, "We need to talk. Put on some walking shoes and we'll trek around the island."

"I had my heart set on going snorkeling," her friend replied, "but okay, let's go for a walk."

Barbie briefly thought of letting Kurt know about their decision, but realizing he was busy getting people and himself ready for diving, she changed her mind. She and Hope would most likely be back before the others were done with their dives.

So the two friends soon were on their way, starting east of the estate, using a rugged path leading all the way around the land mass. Sometimes they got close to the water's edge, now and then veering farther inland where the landscape turned into a perpetual flower paradise. Blooming hedges of hibiscus and bougainvillea vines stretched along the trail. Ginger plants and Java plum trees had spread naturally. The guava tree with its yellow fruits and pink pulp grew in abundance, and the strawberry guava was also common on the island and bore small, edible red fruit. Except for an occasional chirping of birds, there was stillness all around.

A few minutes into their walk, Hope stood still and exclaimed, "This is lovely! No wonder the place is called Isle of Ease."

"Yeah, yeah, the landscape is beautiful," Barbie shot back. "Now cut the crap and tell me what's wrong!"

Equally angry now, Hope shouted, "Don't you see what you've done? The man is almost old enough to be your grandfather!"

"Don't exaggerate; he's only 54."

"That's ancient to us, and you know it. True, he seems in good shape for someone of his generation, but what could you possibly have in common with the man?" She held up an arm before Barbie could reply and continued, "Are you that fond of what money can do for you? And don't bother to tell me you married for love, I won't buy it."

Barbie said, "I admire Kurt. He came from humble beginnings and built up his real estate empire from scratch, earning every dime of his millions with hard work and endurance. He grew up as the oldest in a family of five children, and his folks had a hard time making ends meet. And now he is extremely generous toward his aging parents and siblings."

"You haven't answered my question."

"Okay, so it wasn't love at first sight, but I'm fond of him. I'm positive that he loves me, and with time I'll learn to love him too."

Or hate him, Hope thought, but refrained from speaking up.

They walked in silence for some time. Barbie scanned the ocean with a faraway stare and Hope regretted having been blunt with her friend. After all, she was a guest on this island that belonged to Barbie's husband and had accepted a week's paid vacation from the millionaire. Who was she to judge? Kurt seemed to treat her friend well, and maybe that was all that counted in the long run. I know that I'm overly protective. I would do anything for Barbie - - anything, she thought.

She was pulled out of her reverie when Barbie said, "It isn't the money, you know. Kurt has connections in the entertainment world."

Hope gave her a friendly nudge and said, "I know that getting ahead in your singing career is the most important thing in your life, and I do understand your motivation, but you don't need his clout. After seeing your performance last night, I'm convinced that you could make it big on your own."

They trailed along the north shore, and as they passed a few unoccupied cottages Hope asked, "Isn't Alexa Weller the woman who dumped Kurt?"

"Yeah, don't remind me! I wish I could hex her off the island."

"So what's *she* doing here?"

Before Barbie got a chance to respond, a wild-eyed old man appeared out of nowhere and barred their way.

The hermit yelled, "Go away - - back where you came from!"

Startled, the two young women stopped in their tracks.

The man shook a fist at them and went on, "You people bring wickedness to this peaceful place, with your helicopter stirring up the sacred earth, divers disturbing sea creatures, and loud music intruding the stillness of night."

Hope found enough gumption to say, "Sorry you feel that way."

The hermit stamped his foot and pointed northeast, while shouting his prophecy, *"Leave the island or evil will befall you!"*

He vanished as fast as he had appeared.

Barbie was shaken and said, "Was that a threat?"

"Don't get paranoid," Hope said. "He's a crazy old man. I'd go bananas too if stranded on this tiny island with nobody to talk to."

Some twenty minutes later, when the two friends approached the mansion from the west side, they had made peace with one another.

CHAPTER 12

Meanwhile, Mike and Beatrice Triest enjoyed playing swimming games with Evie. The girl was an excellent swimmer. She never tired of tossing a noodle around and diving for rings at the bottom of the pool. Evie soon had the Triests exhausted and stayed in the water by herself.

When Beatrice stepped out of the pool, she came face to face with Alexa, who had settled in a lounge chair. The former gave the younger woman a dirty look, grabbed her towel from a chair nearby, and then moved all the way to the other end of the pool area, motioning to her husband to do likewise.

Alexa had been racking her brain trying to remember where she had met Mike and Beatrice Triest, ever since the boat ride from Honolulu, when Beatrice had darted murderous looks at her from a distance. Now, seeing her up close, she finally recalled the place and circumstance. A couple of years ago, she had been the defense attorney for the doctor whom the Triests accused of negligence in a malpractice suit, arising out of their son dying from a prescription drug overdose. Alexa won the case, establishing that no negligence or wrongdoing on the part of the physician could be proven. Alexa, in fact, had made

minced meat out of the witnesses for the prosecution and
had used every trick of the trade to get the jurors to arrive
at a favorable verdict for her client.

She had no qualms about it, neither at the time nor
now. A defense attorney is hired to do what it takes to get
his or her client off the hook. She briefly debated whether
she should go after the woman and explain it to her but
changed her mind. It would be useless. All the Triest pair
could think about was that they had lost their son and
needed to blame someone for his death.

Beatrice tried hard to focus all her attention on watching
Evie swim but couldn't stop her rapid heartbeat. Looking
into those arrogant eyes had brought the entire trial back
to her, with all its drama and consequent suffering, as if it
had all happened yesterday. She remembered how, when
the expert witness made a strong point in the prosecution's
favor, Alexa suddenly had an acute asthma attack, and
the judge adjourned the court. On the next day, as that
same witness returned to the stand, sly Alexa had found
a way to contradict his findings. Beatrice teared up as she
glanced over to Mike in the lounge chair next to her and
thought, I wish I hadn't come and doubt that I can stand
being around that woman for a week.

Mike reached over and patted her on the shoulder,
saying, "I know what you're thinking. Don't worry, I'll
make it up to you."

When Evie was done playing in the pool, she climbed
out, wrapped herself in a towel, and went over to the
Triests. She said, "Thanks for keeping me company.
Mommy said I need to shower after swimming. I'm going
up now."

"Need any help?"

"No, I'm independent."

Beatrice watched her leave the pool area and thought, what a mature and delightful child! I hope her mom realizes it, enjoying every precious minute together with her. Kids grow up fast and one never knows what lies ahead. Picturing her own son when he was that age made Beatrice tear up again.

CHAPTER 13

Neal and Kim ended their dive, surfaced, and then made their way to shore. As they walked over the volcanic rock toward the shed, Kim exclaimed, "That was so much fun! We were lucky to see so many fish and other sea creatures. I got a kick out of the large school of fish that moved up and down in total unison."

Neal said, "Those were White-Spotted Damsels. They are easy to recognize with their blackish-blue coloration and white spot on each side of their body. It was cool seeing them in action."

"Except for the most common - - like angelfish, butterflyfish, and wrasses - - I don't know any of these species," Kim admitted. Then she asked, "What were those orange fish with the blue spots that we saw down around the forty-foot depth?"

"Those were a male and female Potter's Angelfish. They live in pairs, or at times, a male will be surrounded by several females."

"Well, isn't that a hoot," she commented, "like the rooster and his hens, and it is even practiced in some human cultures!"

They had a hearty laugh.

Neal unexpectedly asked, "Do you know why your brother invited me here?"

Kim got serious and replied, "I've been wondering about it, too. Kurt is used to everything always going his way and when it doesn't, he holds a grudge. I can't imagine that he has forgiven you for winning the congressional seat he wanted so much." She laughed and remarked, "Looks like he's softening, though, having invited people whom I would have tagged as *taboo*."

"Like Alexa Weller."

"So you know about her?"

"Of course! It was news at the time; the woman who left the Real Estate King at the altar." And he added, "I didn't think they were a good match in the first place."

Kim raised an eyebrow and said, "How do you figure that?"

"I knew Alexa many years ago when we studied together at law school." He grinned. "We even dated for a short time, but she dropped me like a hot potato when something better came along. As I said, Kurt and Alexa did not seem to work as a couple, each being way too bossy."

"Alexa always intimidated me whenever I was around her," said Kim.

"How so?"

"With her striking face, perfect body, and sharp mind, she managed to make me feel inferior. I didn't realize how much I despised the woman until I first saw her again on the boat ride over."

As she finished that sentence, Kim thought, what am I doing, pouring my heart out to this man I hardly know?

Neal said, "There is nothing wrong with your face or body. As for the sharp mind, there are different types of intelligence. Alexa's is the typical, trial attorney's smarts, and I presume that yours is a more subdued kind."

She was glad that he carefully watched his step traversing the rocky terrain and did not look directly at her as she blushed in response to his compliments.

Hiding her embarrassment, she said, "You were a lawyer before becoming a congressman, so is *your* intelligence the obvious kind?"

He laughed and said, "I never saw the inside of a courtroom. I was a corporate lawyer." But unlike Kim, he kept his feelings to himself, not disclosing that Alexa had stolen an internship with a prestigious criminal defense law firm from under his nose. The internship had landed her a foot in the door to place her in the court room, while he ended up stuck in boring business law.

At the shed, they left their empty tanks and equipment, then struggled out of the wetsuits. Kurt and Rafi had beaten them there and were on their way out. Kim overheard Rafi say to her brother, "That was awesome! Felt like old times when we did the Catalina dives together." And she watched as Kurt nodded in remembrance, slinging an arm around the shoulder of his buddy, as the two men left together.

CHAPTER 14

Evie had finished showering and, clearly bored, stepped out onto the balcony off her room. She looked down to the pool area. Mr. and Mrs. Triest had left, but the lady in the gold metallic bikini was still there. Evie watched as she got out of the lounge chair, walked over to the pool's edge, and lowered herself into the water at the deep end. Mommy had said her name was Mrs. Weller and that she and Mr. Weller occupied the guestroom next to theirs.

On the night before, when people were standing around at the garden party, she had heard someone say that Mrs. Weller used to be Uncle Kurt's girlfriend. That must have been a long time ago, because Evie didn't remember ever seeing the fancy lady. Later, during dinner and when Barbie sang, Evie kept glancing over to where Mrs. Weller sat, fascinated. Everything was interesting about her: the elegant blue dress that had made her light-blue eyes sparkle, and the way she'd worn her dark hair piled up high, and most of all, the teasing expression on her face, which was there even while she talked in her deep voice.

The balcony door to the Wellers' room stood wide open. Evie was curious and peeked inside. Evie and her mom's rooms were feminine, especially Evie's, which was done in pastel colors, predominantly pink. The Wellers' guestroom looked modern, devoid of color.

After a quick glance to the pool, making sure the lady was still swimming, Evie sneaked inside the Wellers' domain. A black-and-white comforter covered the king-size bed. Its headboard and footboard were crafted from ebony, and so were the dresser and nightstands. On one wall hung abstract charcoal drawings, and the wall opposite the large dresser was taken up with a floor-to-ceiling mirrored closet.

Evie hardly registered the décor, she was so engrossed with the makeup case which stood on the dresser. The 12-color eyeshadow palette and brush inside the transparent case seemed to beckon, "Come, try me!" With a bad conscience, yet driven by temptation, she opened the case and then applied a light-blue color to her eyelids. The girl got carried away and tried out several different shades. After applying each, she stepped in front of the mirrored wardrobe closet, admiring her handiwork.

Brush in hand, she gave the purple eyeshadow a final touch in front of the mirror, when she heard footsteps in the hallway, getting closer and closer, then coming to a halt by the door. Oh no; I'm in trouble! Evie thought. Mrs. Weller is going to catch me. There was no time to run to the balcony, so she quickly hid inside the closet. She heard the door to the room being opened as she pulled the sliding mirrored door behind her, but did not manage to close it completely, leaving a four-inch gap.

Evie heard nightstand drawers being pulled open and shut again, as if Mrs. Weller was searching for something. To her surprise, she saw through the crack that the person in the room was not Mrs. Weller. The person found the object, which looked like a whistle, in the top drawer of the dresser. It was a rescue inhaler that people with severe asthma used, but Evie did not know that.

The intruder inserted a 1-millimeter drill bit into a pin chuck and then drilled a tiny hole into the inhaler's canister. There was a hissing sound as the pressurized air and the medication escaped all at once. With the dirty job done, the culprit wiped the fingerprints off the inhaler and placed it back into the drawer. The entire deed took less than a minute.

Evie had no idea she was witnessing a murderer in action. All she could do was hope the person would hurry up and leave so that she could get out of her hiding place undetected. She also had a sudden urge to sneeze, and she gave all her attention to squeezing her nostrils shut in order to stifle the sound. When the coast was clear, Evie left the closet and returned the brush to the makeup case and then ran out the balcony door. Seconds later, she stood in front of her own bathroom mirror, washing the eye makeup off, just as she heard her mom return from the dive.

The would-be killer walked out to the hallway full of self-gratification. Yes, it had all worked as planned. There was no telling when and where Alexa would have her next asthma attack, but sooner or later it would happen and her precious inhaler would fail her and she would die. The counter on the rescue inhaler would still show almost full. Most likely, it would be assumed that the device had simply malfunctioned. If anyone noticed the tiny hole in the canister, and the authorities determined foul play, they could never prove who had done it.

CHAPTER 15

As promised, Kim took her daughter snorkeling that afternoon, making Evie forget all about what she witnessed earlier in the day.

Kim had prepared her child already at home for a first snorkeling experience, bought equipment and had her try it out in their condominium's pool. Evie had gotten the hang of snorkeling with ease and was now excited to do real-life exploring of the sea.

Kim found a calm spot near the shore with shallow reefs. At the water's edge, they slipped on their fins, and she made sure the child-size face mask fit Evie well, having her inhale through the nose, which made the mask stick to her face. Then she pulled the strap of the mask over Evie's head and into position. They waded a few yards into the ocean, until waist-deep for the youngster. Evie put her face in the water, breathed through the snorkel until accustomed to it, then started swimming. Kim donned her own snorkeling equipment, and they were ready to explore the exciting sea life.

Right off the bat, they got a glimpse of an Ornate Butterfly fish, feeding off live coral polyps. The six-inch little fellow was magnificent with his orange diagonal stripes. Evie managed to get close enough to notice his beautiful facial features. Another butterfly fish they came across was the Rainbow Butterfly. Although the fish's wide range of colors are not those of the rainbow, they are nonetheless brilliant and spectacular.

Kim was pleasantly surprised at how well Evie took to the snorkeling experience. It turned out that her kid was a natural. To the child's delight, a school of wrasses suddenly followed them. She did not know it, but these fish were looking for feeding opportunities from the disturbances caused by the snorkelers' motions.

Without warning, Evie came face to face with a huge Green Sea Turtle, almost her own size in length, but wider. The creature nearly swam head-on into her but changed course at the last moment, avoiding a collision. Evie was half scared and half thrilled by the encounter, but refrained from making any jerky moves. Kim, swimming right behind her, felt proud of her daughter.

They saw many more turtles, eels and even an octopus. But by far the most impressive sight was a school of about thirty social Pennant fish, with their extraordinary dorsal fins extending way beyond their black and white bodies.

The adventure was so exhilarating that it was easy to lose track of time. Evie did not show any signs of tiring, and the water was relatively warm, plus she would periodically stand up in the shallow ocean to give herself a rest from swimming. Still, after forty minutes of snorkeling, Kim decided it was enough for Evie's first time out.

When they walked on shore, Evie exclaimed, "That was super cool! Can we do it again tomorrow?"

CHAPTER 16

On Monday morning, Kurt took Barbie and all his guests out on a deep-sea fishing expedition on his yacht. Before heading to the boat anchored at the landing, he couldn't help but make another speech.

He announced, "Deep-sea fish are different from shallow-water fish. Shark, tuna, marlin, and swordfish are large and powerful, putting up a fight when caught. But today, we're going out to catch mahi-mahi for tonight's dinner." With a grin he added, "That doesn't mean mahi-mahi are docile, far from it. These acrobats are hardly easy to pull on board. You'll see. Our target fish takes up residence around lobster pots, weed lines, floating timber, dead sea turtles, or anything that provides refuge from larger predators. Since small organisms hang near these floating debris, they also serve mahi-mahi as feeding stations. We'll take advantage of that knowledge."

That said, he led his charge to the cruiser. At the back end of the 65-foot yacht was a large fishing cockpit with a fighting chair and rod holders providing plenty of space for fishing. Forward from it was raised mezzanine seating, offering a place for spectators to watch the action. A ladder to the right of the salon door led to the fly bridge and its helm station with two captain's chairs and state-of-the-art navigation equipment. At the edge of the helm was an L-shaped seating area with room for six or more people. The inside of the boat sported a large salon, dining area, bar, and galley. Down a flight of stairs were the sleeping accommodations: the master stateroom with a king-size bed and a forward stateroom with a queen bed and a twin bunk, each with its own bathroom.

As everyone was settled in the yacht, Kurt navigated his vessel into deeper waters. Heather Ross was thankful for the anti-motion-sickness pill Kurt had dealt out to her and other people prone to seasickness. Their host seemed to think of everything. She was truly enjoying her island vacation. Yesterday's snorkeling had been a new and exciting experience, and now the deep-sea fishing would be another firsthand adventure. And this was only Monday; who knew what lay in store for the rest of the week!

Similar thoughts went through the majority of people's minds, as they rubbed on sunscreen and looked out to the calm sea below the blue sky.

All of a sudden, Hope nudged Barbie, who sat next to her on the mezzanine, and called out, "Look to your left!"

"Ooh's" and "ah's" escaped some of the others, as they too spotted the humpback whales ready to start heading back north after their winter migration. It was a mother and her calf, accompanied by an escort whale. Their sighting was spectacular.

Kurt and Rafi were the only experienced deep-sea anglers on board. Neal, Max, Sidney, and Mike had made it known before heading out to sea that they would be willing to try their hand at the sport. Beatrice and Heather would definitely be content as spectators only, and the rest of the women kept an open mind.

Rafi spotted the first lobster pot and Kurt turned the engine off, drifting toward it. To see if mahi-mahi were at the target, Rafi tossed a handful of sardine chunks in its direction. Sure enough, there was a school of mahi-mahi of various sizes hanging on the pot. Kurt tossed out baitfish chunks, getting the mahi-mahi into a feeding frenzy, while Rafi and Neal used their rods to cast their brightly colored fly into the melee.

Both soon got results and reeled in their catch. Neal's nine-pound fish gave him a bit of a fight, but Kurt helped him with the hook-up, and they got it on board without much drama. Neal proudly held up his catch for all to see and received hi-fives from the men standing nearby. Evie came down from the mezzanine, eager to get a close-up look at the first catch of the day.

Rafi's 18-pounder was another story. The striking, iridescent multi-colored mahi-mahi was not about to surrender easily and took to the air several times during the fight in an acrobatic aerial display. It ran at top speed under water and then surfaced like a rocket into the air. To make sure that the hook did not pull, Rafi followed the fish's flight with the rod tip. After several such maneuvers, the mahi-mahi tired at last, and Rafi managed to hook the fish and lift it into the boat.

They cast off at several more spots during their five-hour cruise, stopping in between to eat lunch, which Hermina had packed for them. All the men and Hope tried their luck at fishing and caught mahi-mahi ranging from 6 to 15 pounds.

Hope's catch was among the larger ones, and she later confessed to Barbie, "I got a rush reeling in and fighting with that energetic creature! I'd better watch out; deep-sea fishing might be addictive."

"You got dirty, sweaty, and soaked. All good reasons I have no desire to try it, in spite of the thrill it gives Kurt," her friend replied.

Back at the mansion, they handed their treasures to Hermina, who broke down the mahi-mahi into fillets by skinning them and taking out their backbone like a regular fishmonger. She planned to grill a good portion of the fillets for that night's dinner, serve them over rice pilaf, and freeze the rest.

CHAPTER 17

Later in the day, Kurt and Rafi went for another scuba dive, a few people chose to snorkel or go for a stroll, but most hung around the pool area.

Max changed into swimming trunks and said to his wife, "I'm off to snorkel. Are you sure you won't give it a try?"

Alexa, who had slipped into silky loungewear, replied, "Not a chance. I've seen enough fish for one day."

"So far, we haven't spent much time together on the isle. If you're going down to the pool, I'll join you when I'm back."

"Remember, I came here to relax after working myself silly before and during my last trial. I'm planning to read the book I brought along."

As soon as he left, Alexa took the spiral staircase to the ground floor and strolled into the kitchen. Hermina, with the help of Domenica and Rosa, was busy packaging the mahi-mahi fillets she was about to store in the freezer.

The cook asked, "Can I help you?"

Alexa ignored her, and turning to Domenica said, "I noticed earlier that you carried a tray with fruit drinks to the people by the pool. I'm staying in my room, but may I have a drink as well?"

"Sure. I'll bring one up."

"Oh, don't bother; I'll carry it myself."

"As you wish," said Domenica, and went over to the punchbowl on the counter and filled her a glass of the chilled punch.

Moments later, Alexa settled into a lounge chair on the balcony off her guestroom with a book titled, *Laugh Until You Burst*. On the rare occasions that time allowed for recreational reading, she made a point of selecting literature that was not heavy or sad. In particular, nothing that pertained to legal matters, crime, trials, or law enforcement.

She did not start reading right away. While stretching out on the chaise longue, sipping the refreshing punch, she let her thoughts roam. Funny how Max remarked that they hadn't spent much time together. What was new about that? They had had nothing to say to one another in the last several months. She chuckled to herself when she recalled his attempt at making love the night before and suddenly was unable to perform. He must have dwelled on my infidelity or some other weird beef of his.

A contented sigh escaped her as she pondered, I'm having a great time, even though a lot of people on the island hate me. A good thing I'm thick skinned and actually see the humor in it. Kurt is cordial and may have even forgiven me, but could be disguising his true feelings. Barbie seems to consider me her rival. How funny is that! The girl is a talented singer, though, no doubt.

She mused further, Kim is as intimidated by me as ever, and for some strange reason, I seem to have a fan in little Evie. And then there's Neal, who pretends he isn't bothered that I snatched away his internship. Mike and

Beatrice Triest don't try to hide their animosity. At least there is honesty in that. Even Domenica, the housekeeper, appears to hold a grudge. Her eyes shot daggers when she handed over the punch. Of course the woman remembers me from the days I was engaged to Kurt. God only knows who else despises me among this weird thrown-together group. Well, I'm having a grand old time regardless.

Presently, Alexa opened her book to the first chapter and was soon immersed in the satirical read. She was laughing out loud when a sudden gust of wind propelled pollen from a peppertree plant in the air, triggering an asthma attack.

She struggled to breathe air in, but it was as if she had a plastic bag over her face. The more she tried to take air in and realized that she couldn't, the more she panicked and made it worse by constricting her breathing tube, causing swelling of the airways, which partially blocked the airflow to her lungs. The sound that escaped her was a painful wheeze, and she felt her heart racing. She fought to take a deep, proper breath, trying to calm herself down, counting slowly, so that she could get air in, but it was no use. She tensed up, her shoulders and back hunched.

With sweat running down her face from stress and exertion, Alexa wrestled herself out of the chair and staggered inside, made it to the dresser, pulled out the top drawer, and grabbed her rescue inhaler, thinking, *I am saved now*. With a last effort, she shook it a couple of times, opened it, and put her mouth around its mouthpiece, taking a slow breath in, while simultaneously squeezing the pump to deliver the dose of medication, and - - nothing happened. The damned thing failed her. Panic stricken, she tried to push down the pump once more, but her airway was fully blocked by then. She became disoriented, her lips turned bluish, and she lost consciousness, collapsing onto the floor.

Max found her an hour later with the rescue inhaler still clutched in her hand. He desperately attempted mouth-to-mouth resuscitation and chest compressions, despite knowing that he was too late and his efforts were useless. Terrified, he opened his door and yelled into the hallway, "Help! Alexa had a fatal attack."

Kim and Evie stepped off the elevator on the second floor, ready to change out of their bathing suits after snorkeling, when they heard his cry for help.

As Kim peered into the room and saw Alexa sprawled on the floor, lifeless, she quickly blocked her child's view and ordered, "Go to our rooms and stay there until I come back." Then she went in search of her brother.

CHAPTER 18

Kurt's immediate thought was, leave it to Alexa to die on my island and ruin everyone's fun in the sun. Outwardly, however, he took control and did everything by the book. He knew that with any unexpected death, the authorities needed to be contacted right away, so he called 911. At first, there was a bit of an issue about who, exactly, was in charge. The Isle of Ease was under USA's jurisdiction, but since there had never been cause for any member of the executive branch to set foot on the small piece of land, it was not immediately clear from where to dispatch said authorities. In the end, they flew in by helicopter from Honolulu.

There was nothing left for the paramedics to do but lift Alexa's corpse onto a stretcher and load it into the chopper after the coroner had done his preliminary examination. He concluded that the woman had suffocated from an obstruction of the airways due to an acute asthma attack. Whether she was too far gone to activate the pump on her rescue inhaler or the device malfunctioned and failed to release medication for some reason remained to be determined. In any event, he was not about to sign a death certificate until he'd performed an autopsy.

The coroner told Max that the post-mortem would take place in Honolulu and that someone would contact him once the body was released.

Max seemed to be in shock and just nodded.

Detective Kuwada had no reason to treat the case as anything other than an unfortunate accidental death. He had one of his subordinates drop the rescue inhaler and the empty glass found on the balcony into evidence bags, expressed his condolences, and took his leave with the rest of the officials via helicopter.

At dinner, the guests were subdued, and didn't have much appetite, despite the tasty mahi-mahi Hermina and her helpers served. Conversations were strained, and people avoided eye-contact with Max.

Toward the end of the meal, Kurt rose and gave another speech, this one in somber tones. He first spoke to Max and said, "I am so sorry for your loss. Alexa and I may have had our differences in the past, but I invited the two of you here to show that there remained no hard feelings on my part. I hope that I was able to convey that to her." He cleared his throat and continued, "As to the practical aspect. If you decide to go over to Honolulu and wait there until they release her body, I'd be happy to take you on my yacht."

"Let me think on it," Max replied, appearing to be numb.

Kurt went on with his monolog, addressing all his guests now. "Naturally, Alexa's passing is tragic, and I couldn't blame you if you decided to cut your stay here short. In that case I would also take you to Hawaii and make arrangements to reschedule your return flights. But think about it! Leaving serves no purpose. We can't change what happened. I knew Alexa well, and she would want you all to enjoy the rest of your time here."

Barbie thought, he's giving the guests the option to cut their stay short. I wish I was that lucky. I'm sure the proposition doesn't apply to me and I have to stick it out until Friday.

People spent the rest of the evening taking advantage of the many activities in the game room, but no one's heart was in it. Most turned in early and mulled over whether to stay or take Kurt up on his offer to get them home ahead of schedule. Max went up to the gym, trying to work out his sorrow on the exercise machines.

CHAPTER 19

Max was working up a sweat running on the treadmill and thought, what's the use of hanging out in Honolulu? I don't know a soul there and am hardly in the mood to do the tourist thing. I can make arrangements from here and send out e-mails to family and friends. And then it hit him: I have to plan her funeral and let her folks know. God help me!

On the floor below, Kim was kissing her daughter good-night.

Evie asked, "Mommy, can we stay, please?"

"I haven't made up my mind yet."

"Remember what Uncle Kurt said, Mrs. Weller would have wanted us to keep having fun."

"I'm not sure about that."

Evie's eyelids started to droop when she asked, "Did you like her?"

Taken by surprise, Kim replied, "I'm not sure about that either. Good night, my inquisitive angel."

Already half asleep, Evie murmured, "Well, I sure did. She was cool!"

Neal was flossing his teeth and thought, I'll play it by ear. If most people call it quits, I'll head on home too. Being honest with himself, he knew that it mainly depended on Kim. Diving with her had been the highlight of his stay so far and he wanted to repeat the experience. He was drawn to the athletic woman and sensed that the attraction was mutual. Under different circumstances, he would ask her out. The realization stunned him; he'd lost his dear wife less than a year ago.

Sidney and Heather Ross sat out on the balcony sipping their daiquiris and enjoying the tropical evening.

"Are you okay with us staying put?" Sidney asked.

"You bet! It's unfortunate about Alexa, but we hardly knew her."

"That's settled then. Let's enjoy the rest of the week."

The Triests were in bed and Beatrice had trouble falling asleep. She turned from side to side, rearranged her pillow several times, and counted sheep for the umpteenth time, to no avail. Her tossing disrupted Mike's rest too.

He muttered, "Trouble sleeping because of Alexa?"

"That's right," his spouse admitted, "I have a bad conscience."

Suddenly fully awake, he turned on the light, sat straight up in bed, and questioned, "Why on earth do *you* have a bad conscience?"

"As Christians, we have to forgive our enemies. I did not forgive her while she was alive, and now it's too late."

"If you ask me, the woman got what she deserved. God punishes the wicked."

Beatrice did not comment. She believed in a kind and forgiving God, but knew it was useless to argue with Mike about it. Instead she said, "Tomorrow, I'm going to try to comfort her poor husband. I'll think of an act of kindness to help ease his pain."

That said, she switched off the light and was finally able to sleep.

As Rafi came out of the bathroom, Kate ended her call home and said, "All is well with our boys. They said hi."

"It's already past midnight in L.A. Why did they call?"

"I'm the one who made the call, forgetting about the three-hour time difference. So I'm guilty of waking them up."

"Did you tell them what happened here?"

"No. I see no reason why they should know at this point. We can tell them once we're home."

"Good call!" Then he said, "We haven't discussed what to do."

"There's nothing to discuss. Like you, I also want to stay."

"You're amazing! How did you know that's what I want?"

She smiled at him and remarked, "I make it my business to know what's going on in that head of yours."

"You're a dangerous woman!" he said with a chuckle. Then he came closer and gave her "the look" and it did not take a psychic to read what went on in his mind.

Hope mulled over that afternoon's event. She had not known Alexa prior to meeting her on the island. Even here, she hardly came in contact with the woman. She had known *of* her and that she was a highly successful defense attorney, remembering a high-profile case the lawyer had won a couple of years earlier. Observing Alexa in the short time on the isle, she noticed that the woman had excellent taste in clothing, good looks, self-confidence beyond measure, a sense of humor, an unusually deep voice, and an arrogant attitude. It was paradox that such a triumphant human being had been vulnerable to asthma attacks and in the end succumbed to one of them. Although distressing, Alexa's death did not affect Hope personally.

Her last thought before she dosed off was, no way will I miss out on any adventures on this island. I'm staying until Friday.

CHAPTER 20

First thing on Tuesday morning, Detective Kuwada found the deceased woman's rescue inhaler and the glass he had submitted for analysis, together with the lab report he had requested, on his desk. Fast work! he noted. I'm lucky to have an excellent team at my disposal.

The report read, *"No malfunction of the inhaler's pump detected. According to the marker on the counter, which is at the number 110, the canister should be more than two-thirds full. In reality, it is empty. Upon close examination, there is a minute hole on the inside wall of the canister. All medication must have escaped through that cavity. As to the glass: only residue of fruit punch was found, no other substance."*

Detective Kuwada thought, I didn't expect any other findings in or on the glass, but it never hurts to be thorough.

Then he put on a pair of latex gloves, picked up the inhaler, pulled the casing off, and inspected the canister. Sure enough, there was a tiny hole, barely noticeable, unless one was looking for it. He thought to himself, interesting! We are looking at a murder investigation now. And as he took the gloves off, he realized that they would not have been needed. The dusting for fingerprints had already taken place and was found useless. In addition to the victim's, there had been numerous prints on the device interfering with each other.

He stared at the numbers on the counter of the inhaler, deep in thought. Then he nodded to himself and reached for his phone.

Max Weller had been awake most of the night, but finally dosed off in the early morning. He was groggy when answering the phone after several rings.

"Good morning, Mr. Weller. Detective Kuwada here."

"Hello. Are you releasing my wife's body?"

"Not just yet. The coroner has not completed the autopsy."

"Oh," Max said, disappointed.

"I'm calling because I have a question. When did your wife have an asthma attack last? I don't mean the one she had on the island."

Fully awake now, Max didn't have to think about it, and said, "It was last November, the day before Thanksgiving. We were about to drive to the airport and fly to the East Coast to visit my wife's parents. As we walked to our detached garage, the neighbor's gardener was mowing their lawn. Alexa is - - I mean was - - highly allergic to grass, and it triggered the attack."

"And after using the rescue inhaler she was fine?"

"She was a bit shaken but could breathe again."

"Okay. So that was over four months ago. Do you know if at that time she used the same inhaler as yesterday?"

"Yes, she did."

"Are you sure?"

"Positive. When packing it to take on the island, she even mentioned that it was practically full since she'd only used it that one time. Why is that important?" he asked with an edge to his voice.

Detective Kuwada was evasive with his answer. "It may or may not be," he said. Then he thanked him and ended the call.

The information left the detective with plenty of food for thought. Somebody had tampered with that inhaler after its use in November. He supposed that the deed had been done on the island, which would include everyone at the mansion as suspect. Unless, of course, the husband was the guilty party, and it could have been done at any time in the last four months.

He examined the canister once more. It was made from stainless steel. There was no mention in the report what tool could have possibly been used to poke a hole, but obviously a simple jab with a sharp object would not do. The tiny opening must have been achieved with a small drill. So there was careful planning involved; no one would just happen to have such a drill handy on the Isle of Ease.

The people staying at Kurt Nobel's mansion needed to undergo his scrutiny as soon as he could obtain their names. For now, he'd start with the victim's husband, Max Weller.

CHAPTER 21

In mid-morning, Detective Kuwada, impeccably dressed in a suit and tie, together with two of his subordinates in uniform - - one a woman, the other a man - - arrived once more by helicopter. This time, unannounced and with a search warrant.

Most guests were having breakfast in the dining room, or lingered there, not yet knowing what to do on this day that followed a tragedy. Some had gone up to their rooms to change into bathing suits.

Kurt hurried outside and intercepted the law enforcement group as soon as the chopper blades stopped spinning. Slightly out of breath, he asked, "What's up, officers?"

Detective Kuwada stated, "I'm afraid we are looking at a homicide now."

Kurt was speechless.

"Please keep this quiet at present. I'd like to talk to the victim's husband first."

"Sure."

"In the meantime, I'd appreciate if you would assemble all people in one room. I need to make an announcement."

They were walking toward the mansion now and the detective continued, "I have a search warrant with me."

"What the devil for?"

"I'll explain in due course. Also, I'll need to interview each person separately. Maybe you can assign me a room for that purpose."

"The den is probably most convenient. I'll show you the way."

Kurt managed to keep everyone in the dining room, and with the help of Domenica, gathered the people who had already left, except for Max, who was a no-show at breakfast. While Kurt tried to pacify his guests - - some of them demanding to know what had happened - - Detective Kuwada knocked on Max's guest bedroom door and was told to come in.

The man he found in his bathrobe sitting on the unmade bed looked pathetic, but the detective was too professional to let that influence him.

"More questions?" Max said, showing little interest.

"Just a few, Mr. Weller. According to the information I have, your business is in generic drugs and medical patents, correct?"

"That's right."

"I take it that you're familiar with rescue inhalers for asthma."

"Yes, from a professional aspect, as well as a personal one. My wife has used inhalers ever since I've known her."

"Do you know where she stored the inhaler here on the island?"

"She kept it in the top drawer of the dresser."

"Yesterday, when you found your wife, did you examine the inhaler?"

Max stared, then shook his head.

Detective Kuwada stated, "I'm sorry to have to inform you that your wife's case has turned into a homicide investigation. Someone tampered with her inhaler."

Max burst out, "You're telling me Alexa was murdered?"

"That is correct." He gave the man time to digest the fact and then asked, "Do you have any idea who could have wanted your wife dead?"

"Alexa is - - was - - a defense attorney and naturally made enemies. But murder? No way!"

Detective Kuwada knew what the woman's profession had been since he'd checked her background earlier, but just said, "I see."

Max blurted, "I don't feel so good. Is that all?"

"I understand. Only one more question. Other people aside, did *you* have a less-than-harmonious relationship with your spouse?"

Max stared at the wall opposite his bed, clearly in a world of his own. When his eyes finally focused on the detective, they were moist and he said, "We had our differences, but I loved her."

CHAPTER 22

Detective Kuwada's announcement to the assembled group was basically what he had already told Kurt and Max, namely that the authorities no longer considered Alexa's death accidental and were treating it as a homicide investigation. As the detective continued, it became clear that leaving the island was no longer an option. In fact, at the moment they seemed to be prisoners in the dining room.

He stated, "It is necessary to conduct a search of the mansion, including all the guestrooms, as well as the quarters of the domestic employees. At the same time, I will interview each person separately in the den. So please stay here in the dining room until you are called, and return to it again after your interviews. While you are waiting for your turn to be questioned, think in detail about each day since you arrived on this island. If you witnessed anything unusual, no matter how trivial it seems, you need to let me know."

He motioned to his male subordinate and the man left, obviously to search the place. The woman in uniform stayed put, doubtless to babysit the guests.

"Thank you all for your cooperation. I'm heading to the den now." And with a nod at Kurt, he said, "I'll start with you, Mr. Nobel."

As soon as the detective and Kurt left, Evie asked, "Mommy, what is the policeman searching for?"

"I have no idea, Sweetie."

"Can we at least go to the game room?"

"You heard what the detective said, we need to stay here. But I'll make an exception and let you play games on my smartphone."

"Cool!" Evie said, instantly content.

The rest of the group was not that easily gratified. They grunted and complained, but were left no choice but to settle in the dining room for what may well be a long time. When Max joined them, the other guests became tongue-tied. It was obvious that he suffered, and it would have been rude to stare at him.

In the den, Detective Kuwada mentioned to Kurt that their conversation was being recorded as he turned the device on. He started the interview by saying, "Mr. Nobel, yesterday, you told me that the people here are your guests. At that time there was no need to ask for specifics; it was none of my business. Things have changed. Now I make it my business to know. Why have you invited these folks to stay on your island?"

Kurt explained.

"Congratulations! So the people here are family and close friends?"

"Our immediate family and closest friends attended the actual wedding. My guests here are colleagues, acquaintances, friends, and yes, even a former rival. My youngest sister and little niece are also here, since she couldn't make it to the wedding."

There was a cold undertone in Kurt's voice as he said, "Before you go on, detective, I demand to know why this has turned into a homicide investigation."

Detective Kuwada calmly told him about the hole in the canister of Alexa's inhaler. And when Kurt glared at him openmouthed but without comment, he continued the questioning, "When did your guests arrive, and how long are they planning to stay?"

"They came on Saturday, and they'll be staying until Friday."

"Did they all know one another before coming to the island?"

"Some did, but as far as I know, most of them had not met before."

"What about Alexa Weller. Did your guests know her beforehand?"

Kurt replied, "Same applies to Alexa; some did and others didn't."

"How far in advance did your guests learn about your celebration here?"

"I sent out the invitations in February."

"Did you notice any animosity shown toward Alexa Weller on the part of your visitors?"

"Not at all. Everyone got along just fine."

"What was your own relationship with the victim?"

"We were friends. In fact, I was once engaged to Alexa."

Detective Kuwada could not hide his surprise and said, "You astonish me, sir. Inviting a former fiancée to your wedding celebration!"

Kurt said, "I wanted to show that there were no hard feelings." And he became somber as he continued, "Now I wish that I hadn't and she would still be alive."

"How would you describe the kind of person Alexa Weller was?"

"She was a brilliant attorney, but you probably want a more personal account."

The detective nodded.

Without hesitation Kurt said, "Alexa was a fascinating woman: smart, stunning face and body, and she had an uncanny wit."

"What do you mean by 'uncanny wit'?"

"She found humor in just about anything and had a tendency to mock people."

"When did your engagement to Ms. Weller came to an end?"

"Six years ago."

"May I ask who broke it up?"

"Sure, it's no big secret. Alexa did."

Interesting woman, Detective Kuwada thought. Aloud he said, "And you two kept in contact over the last six years?"

"Not frequently. But, yes, we did occasionally. We had some mutual acquaintances and met socially, and she also recommended a couple of good business lawyers when I had the need for them."

"Did you know that she suffered from asthma and used an inhaler?"

"Yes, of course. She had the condition already when we dated."

The detective changed the subject and said, "I understand that you have employees here."

"One of my guests is my CFO. As for the domestics, our housekeeper, her helper, and our cook came along. There is also a gardener and pool maintenance guy."

"That's all the questions I have for the moment." And handing him a pad and pen, he added, "Do me a big favor and list everyone's name, starting with your bride, your guests, and ending with the domestic employees."

As Kurt jotted down his list, Detective Kuwada mulled over their interview. So the killer had had since February to plan and prepare the crime. More than enough time. It was interesting to learn that the newlywed was once engaged to the victim. Millionaires must make their own rules of etiquette, he mused, wondering how Nobel's new wife felt about it.

Having finished the list, Kurt was excused and the detective asked him to send Barbie in when he got back to the dining room.

CHAPTER 23

Detective Kuwada thought, contrary to common belief, homicide detective work is mostly tedious. Granted, there is the occasional exciting chase, the exhilaration when finding evidence and proof that one is on the right track, and the satisfaction that a criminal will be brought to justice. But there is nothing glamourous or thrilling about interviewing suspects. Posing more or less the same questions to person after person is monotonous and time consuming. Yet it remains the only way to arrive at what happened by feeling out each suspect. Sometimes a person's lie could be just as revealing as the truth.

Before each person stepped inside the den to be interviewed, he quickly referred to Mr. Nobel's list and explored their backgrounds. Regardless, once they were seated, he asked for and recorded their personal data, such as address and phone number. So far, he had questioned Barbie Nobel, Kim Frederique - - he decided to skip talking with her daughter for now - - Hope De Luca, and Neal Victor.

The detective had been curious about Barbie. He'd heard her songs on the radio but had never seen her, not even in a photo. He had pictured her older. The young woman before him looked barely out of high school. Barbie had been evasive when asked how she felt about the ex-fiancée of her husband. He believed her statement that she had met Alexa Weller for the first time on the Isle of Ease. On the other hand, he suspected that claiming she didn't know about her asthma was a lie. Other than that, he had not learned anything new from her.

Kim Frederique's account of what had happened on the isle, was straightforward. Her words, "I am so sorry that a happy celebration turned into tragedy," seemed sincere. She freely admitted that Alexa had never been on her "favorite person list," and also that she knew about the victim's frequent asthma attacks.

Hope De Luca was a mature and levelheaded young woman, in his opinion. If anyone could pull off a successful, undetected murder, he would bet his money on her. Yet he did not see any reason she would have had to kill the victim. She was the bride's friend, had never met any of the other guests prior to this trip, and had not known about Alexa's asthma.

Neal Victor's interview had been interesting. It soon became clear what Kurt Nobel had meant by "his former rival." It was noteworthy that the man had also dated the victim at one time in the past. He even admitted that part of the reason he accepted the Nobels' invitation, was because he was curious about her. Detective Kuwada reflected that it might have been interesting to have known Alexa Weller alive. She must have had some magnetism to be pulling men's strings years after the relationships ended. Neal Victor acknowledged to have known about the asthma. He was also the first suspect, aside from Kurt Nobel, who questioned why dying from a fatal asthma attack had suddenly turned into a murder investigation. Without giving any specifics, the detective had informed him that there was evidence the victim's inhaler had been tampered with.

The next person to be interviewed was Sidney Ross. Detective Kuwada had a personable way to start each questioning. To this suspect he said, "I see you are Mr. Nobel's CFO. You must also be his friend, having been invited to the island party."

"You've got that right."

Before the detective could continue, Sidney asked, "What do you expect your man to find with this room search?"

"Funny, you're the first person inquiring. We are seeking a certain tool, but that is all I'm willing to disclose at this time."

The routine questioning progressed, and Detective Kuwada learned that Sidney had first met the victim years ago, when she was engaged to his boss, but never knew her well. He had been aware of her asthma affliction, since his boss had mentioned it on several occasions. Sidney elaborated on one particular such attack that Kurt Nobel had told him about.

Only half-heartedly paying attention, the detective's thoughts lingered on the search his subordinate was conducting, since the current suspect had brought it up. In his opinion, the endeavor would most likely be unsuccessful. If the culprit was not a complete idiot, the murder weapon was at the bottom of the ocean by now. But of course, they had to go through the motion.

He asked his last question, "Did you like Alexa Weller?"

Sidney took his time before he answered, "She was a stunning woman with plenty of sex appeal. Even being middle aged with grown kids, I was attracted. It would take a blind man not to be." He paused, then added, "But no, I did not *like* her."

"Thank you for your honesty, Mr. Ross," said the detective and ended the interview.

Heather Ross was next, and her answers were mostly unremarkable. She hardly knew the victim, but had heard about her asthma attacks. When asked her opinion of Alexa Weller, she mentioned, "The woman had a lovely figure and clothes to die for." Then realizing her faux pas, quickly added, "Sorry, that was a poor choice of words."

Although Heather Ross was a charming lady, she had nothing new to contribute to the investigation, and Detective Kuwada thanked and dismissed her.

He was still doing the background check on Rafi Simonian, when the latter entered the den.

He looked up and said, "Have a seat, Mr. Simonian. I see that you're listed as entrepreneur. What kind of business do you own?"

"I've started and sold many businesses over the last twenty years. I retailed everything from vertical blinds to lamp shades."

"All profitable, I hope."

Rafi smiled and replied, "Some highly, and others not so much. Last month, I patented my newest product: novelty sunglass frames. If you're interested, I can give you a brochure."

Amused, the detective continued the interview. He learned that Rafi Simonian's friendship with Kurt Nobel went back to the days their sons played on the same soccer team as small boys. Questioned about his relationship with the victim, the man stated that he had only met her once prior to coming to the island, which was years ago. When asked if he knew about the asthma, Rafi's reply was that he only learned of it on Sunday in the shed when Alexa backed out of her decision to snorkel. To the question about his opinion of her, he grinned and said, "She was hot, and from what I heard a top-notch attorney, but I don't think she had soul, if you know what I mean."

There goes an interesting man, the detective thought, as Rafi walked out the den.

CHAPTER 24

Kate Simonian had barely sat down to be questioned, when the housekeeper stuck her head in the door and addressed the detective, "Sorry to interrupt. I'm Domenica Cortes. Hermina is preparing lunch and we'll serve it in fifteen minutes. I have set an extra table for you and your officers: Señor Nobel invites you for the meal."

"That is generous. Thank you!" He had planned to eat an energy bar, but a real lunch was a welcome surprise.

To Kate he said, "Okay, let's get started. I understand that you write mystery novels."

"Correct. Do you like reading the genre?"

"Lord no! When off duty, I want to have nothing to do with crime or criminals."

"I hear you."

Then he posed the questions which had become second nature to him. He learned that Kate had never met Alexa Weller before the trip to the Isle of Ease, nor had she known about her asthma disorder. Her estimation of the victim was the following, "You saw Alexa dead and I don't know what she looked like then, but alive she was a striking beauty." Smiling, she added, "I take it you want a less superficial account. Well, I found her witty and amusing."

He was about to end the interview but got curious and said, "I see you carry a tablet. Are you working on a new book?"

"At home I am, but here I'm just keeping a journal."

"May I have a look at it? It may help with my investigation."

She said, "Oh, it's just some observations I jotted down. Nothing important," but selected the app with the journal and handed him the tablet. It read:

"Saturday, April 8:

The flight from LAX to Honolulu was uneventful, and we had a calm sea on the boat ride over. Some of the passengers, though, looked far from being calm. One could have cut the bad vibes in the air with a knife! The animosity seemed to be directed toward an attractive woman, wearing chic clothing. Rafi pointed out that she was Alexa Weller. Especially one of the older couples - - we haven't been introduced yet - - gave the woman the evil eye.

Our 'home' for the next week is a lovely castle, straight out of a fairytale book. From the outside, that is. Once one steps indoors, the place transfers into a modern mansion with every comfort imaginable. Our room is attractive: large, airy, and the décor shows good taste. I've already tried out the Jacuzzi jets in the bathroom!

At the garden party, we were treated to a fabulous barbecue prime rib dinner. We first mingled with the other guests and learned that the couple I mentioned before is Mike and Beatrice Triest. Sidney and Heather Ross are middle aged with grown children. My goodness! I just realized that Rafi and I are considered middle aged too! Of course we recognized Congressman Neal

Victor, even though we had not previously met. Kurt's sister Kim, and her little girl are here too. I do remember her from the time she used to come watch the boys' soccer games.

Barbie's friend Hope seems to be a mature and remarkable young woman. She is planning to major in computer science. At dinner, Alexa and Max Weller joined our table. The woman has style, as well as wit. As to her husband, he seems to be the quiet type. Whether out of shyness or caution is hard to determine. The highlight of the evening was an amazing performance by Kurt's bride. There is more to Barbie than I thought. The young woman's got talent.

Sunday, April 9:

Went snorkeling with the Ross pair and Max Weller. They all are accomplished snorkelers, whereas I am not. My first crack at the activity was indeed an experience. I loved every minute of it. When walking back from the shed, I observed something funny. I saw little Evie coming onto the balcony from her room, and then she vanished into the adjacent guestroom. As I got closer to the mansion a bit later, she appeared again and then ran back into her own bedroom. The child must have found a way to amuse herself! Her secret is safe with me.

Rafi was back from scuba diving and taking a shower when I reached our room, and I was just in time to freshen up too, before lunch was served in the dining room. Needless to say, the food tasted excellent. In the afternoon, Rafi and I went for a stroll. The estate immediately around the house is kept in perfect tropical order - - trimmed shrubs and trees - - but farther away, the island has a wild, untamed beauty.

Monday, April 10:

What a tragic day! While Rafi is fast asleep, I'm trying to recapture the events.

The day started pleasant, full of adventure. Early in the morning, Kurt took us deep-see fishing. Right off the bat, we got treated to a bit of whale watching. What a spectacular sight! That alone would have made worth the sea trip, but watching the anglers catching mahi-mahi was a new adventure for me. I never went along on Rafi's previous fishing excursions, and although happy with the tasty catches he brought home, I didn't understand his love of the sport. Now I get it!

In mid-afternoon, Kurt and Rafi went scuba diving again, and many of us swam in, or relaxed around the pool. When looking up to the castle, I noticed Alexa out on her balcony. Little did I know that apparently shortly afterwards, she took in her last breath. Her husband found her dead and beyond help. She had expired from a fatal asthma attack. Bad news travels fast. I don't remember who sounded the alarm, but those of us in the pool area learned about it promptly.

At dinner, our host gave a speech. He didn't manage to cheer anyone up, but got us thinking whether or not we should stay or cut the trip short. Later, people tried to get a sense of normalcy in the game room, but the general atmosphere was gloomy. I, for one, tried to have fun with Ms Pacman but didn't succeed.

Tuesday, April 11:

A good thing I grabbed my tablet when the housekeeper announced that we had to go back to the dining room. It looks like we're trapped here for a long time.

I can't imagine what the search is all about. I mean, the woman had an asthma attack; they can't be looking for a murder weapon. Could they possibly be hunting for something that triggered her condition? Or maybe she did not have an attack at all and the autopsy showed a different cause of death. This is all speculation, of course. Detective Kuwada - - with Hawaiian good looks - - was pleasant enough with his announcement, as he called it, but told us nothing beyond that he is conducting a murder investigation.

In my fictional murder tales, I can shape everything and everyone to my liking and make it all fit, while dishing out clues which may or may not enlighten the reader. This being a real-life murder, I am kept in the dark like all other guests. I don't like the feeling!

I'm looking around this room, searching people's faces, trying to figure out their reactions to what has happened on this peaceful stretch of land that we are now stuck on. What I see is fear, insult, contempt, but mostly…"

Here the journal broke off.

Detective Kuwada handed the tablet back and stated, "You are extremely observant."

"Comes with the territory," she replied.

There was mirth in his voice when he acknowledged, "Thank you for the 'Hawaiian good looks.' And what was that last word you wanted to write when you got interrupted, obviously to be asked to talk with me?"

She checked the last entry on her journal and said, "I meant to write 'annoyance'. I think most people are annoyed about the room search and being detained."

"Understandable." Then he checked his watch and said, "Time for lunch."

CHAPTER 25

Lunch was a simple menu of French dip with asparagus on the side. None of the guests seemed hungry, though. Sitting on the same chair, in the same room for hours, was not consistent with working up an appetite. The conversations were strained, in part because of what had happened to Alexa, and to some extent due to the law enforcers present. In contrast, Detective Kuwada and his subordinates dug in with gusto.

What had occurred at the beginning of the meal at their table did not pass unnoticed by the guests in the dining room. The officer who had conducted the search handed Detective Kuwada a brown evidence bag, while speaking to him in a soft voice. The detective was surprised, not having expected the room search to produce any results, but his face stayed expressionless. Naturally, people wondered what and where evidence could have been discovered. One person was the exception and knew precisely what was in the bag and where it had been found.

Before dessert was served, Detective Kuwada stood up and told the assembled group, "You are free to leave the dining room now, but must stay on the island. The exceptions are Mr. and Mrs. Triest, whom I still need to interview. I would also like to have a talk with each of the domestic staff. Oh, and Mr. Victor, would you please also stick around. We need to have another word."

He looked at his watch and said, "Give me about twenty minutes; I need to confer with my team, and then we are ready to continue the interviews. It doesn't matter in which order you come to the den."

Detective Kuwada used the twenty minutes to catch his subordinates up with what he had learned from each suspect's interview that morning. He mentioned Kate's journal, and stated the highlights of it, as much as he'd memorized.

His female officer said, "This is a carefully premeditated crime. There is no way the culprit could have tampered with the victim's inhaler on the spur of the moment. That means we have to concentrate on the people who knew the victim beforehand. So far, that would exclude Barbie Nobel, Hope De Luca, and Kate Simonian."

"I agree, assuming all three told the truth," said Detective Kuwada.

"According to her husband, Alexa Weller kept the rescue inhaler in their guest bedroom in her dresser's top drawer. The killer must have sneaked into the couple's room to drill that hole into the canister of the inhaler."

"Correct. I've also come to that conclusion," said Detective Kuwada.

"The male officer asked, "Sir, do you find Ms. Simonian's journal helpful with our investigation?"

"It may be. In any event, the journal is extremely interesting."

"You mean her mentioning that the older couple, Mike and Beatrice Triest, seem to have hated Alexa Weller?"

"That too, but I was thinking of what she had observed about the child. It could mean something, or it may have nothing to do with the case."

"What about the evidence I found? Are we going to treat the person occupying that room as our prime suspect?"

"Let's wait and hear what the individual has to say. And now I had better research the Triests, before they show up."

CHAPTER 26

Exactly twenty minutes had elapsed since the law enforcers left the dining room, when Beatrice Triest knocked on the den's door. Detective Kuwada got up and met her at the doorway, then escorted her to the sofa and took a seat in his upright chair, facing her. His two underlings moved farther back in the room and also sat down. One opened his laptop, ready to take notes, while the other got busy with the recording device.

Detective Kuwada said, "You are a homemaker, correct?"

"That's right."

"I understand that you also volunteer and organize charitable events."

She nodded and said, "It is my way of giving back to the community. I find it emotionally gratifying."

"Now let's get to the matter at hand. Did you know Alexa Weller before this gathering here on the island?"

"Yes, I did, and it was not a happy occasion."

The detective waited, not uttering a word, knowing there was more to come.

Beatrice continued, "One should not talk ill of the dead, but I can't help holding the woman responsible for never getting justice and closure in the premature passing of my son."

"So sorry to hear that. How was Alexa Weller involved in your son's death?"

"She was the defense attorney for the doctor in our malpractice suit. We accused him of negligence in the care of our son, which killed our Mickey. The doctor was acquitted due to her misleading several witnesses." A lone tear rolled down her cheek as she stated, "I know the doctor's conviction wouldn't have brought Mickey back, but at least we'd have gotten justice."

Detective Kuwada said, "I can understand your frustration, but as the physician's defense attorney, Ms. Weller only did her job."

"I didn't care and hated her!" she burst out. And there was a full stream of tears as she divulged, "And now she's dead and I'm too late to forgive her."

There was a tissue box on the end table next to the sofa. The detective reached over and silently handed it to her.

She dabbed her eyes, blew her nose, and pulled herself together.

Detective Kuwada carried on with his questioning, "Did you know that Alexa Weller suffered from asthma and used rescue inhalers?"

"I sure did. She had an attack during the trial and used an inhaler. At the time I thought that she conveniently staged the episode during the testimony of an expert witness. Now I feel guilty for having jumped to that conclusion. Her attack must have been genuine."

At that point the detective ended the interview, before the lady had a chance to start another crying spell.

As soon as she was out the door, he asked his staff, "What did you think of her statements?"

One officer said, "I feel sorry for her. She's tormenting herself with guilt for having hated the victim."

The other remarked, "Or she's a clever actress, trying to suggest that fact to us."

Detective Kuwada was prevented from giving his own impression when Mike Triest appeared.

He started by saying, "So you are Mr. Nobel's real estate business colleague."

"The term *competitor* is more accurate. We tend to compete with one another for real estate development."

"Yet he invited you to celebrate on his island?"

"I was as surprised as you seem to be when I got the invitation," Mike remarked with a twinkle in his eye.

"Now to our investigation. We've already learned from your wife that Alexa Weller was the defense attorney in a malpractice trial where the doctor, who treated your son, was the defendant. The court's ruling was in the doctor's favor, resulting in Mrs. Triest harboring strong feelings against Ms. Weller. Did you share those same feelings?"

"Naturally, I was also mad at Alexa Weller. I understand that it was her job to use any trick of her trade to get the bastard off the hook, but at the end of the day, we didn't get justice for our son."

He paused, and then added, "I blame her most of all for what she did to my wife. Beatrice has not been the same woman ever since the trial. She has trouble sleeping, bursts into tears at the drop of a hat, and has even lost all interest in sex."

It was obvious that the man had worked himself into a rage, and while the detective searched for the right words to calm him down, Mike continued, "I sure hope she gets back to normal, now that the Weller woman is dead."

Following all that ranting, the detective decided not to ask about the asthma and inhaler. From Mrs. Triest's statement, he already knew that the couple had witnessed one of Ms. Weller's major attacks in court. Instead, he asked, "Did you know before coming here that Alexa Weller was going to be one of the guests?"

"She was on the list, but I doubted that she'd show up."

"What list is that?"

"The Nobels attached a guest list to their invitation."

"That is news to me. Nobody else mentioned that list." Detective Kuwada grinned and said, "I must not have asked the right question."

Then he thanked Mike Triest for his honesty and let him go.

As the door closed behind him, one of the officers said, "Sir, do you think the guest list thing is important?"

"To me it sure is," said Detective Kuwada. "Until now, I was puzzled as to how the murderer knew in advance that Alexa Weller would be one of the guests. With the existence of that list, *everybody* knew!"

Another knock at the door cut their talk short.

CHAPTER 27

"You wanted to see me again?" Neal asked.

"Please have a seat, Mr. Victor. I'll try to make this quick. You can imagine what the result of our search amounts to."

"I haven't got a clue."

"You may recall that when you questioned the homicide investigation earlier, I informed you that Ms. Weller's inhaler had been tampered with."

"Yes, of course."

"We found the tool!"

Neal stared at him, not seeming to understand.

Detective Kuwada continued, "Guess what we came across inside your suitcase?"

Neal protested, "My suitcase is empty. I unpacked it Saturday upon arrival and tucked it away in the back of the closet."

The detective reached behind his chair and grabbed the brown evidence bag. Pulling the transparent bag out of it and holding it up, he said, "What about this?"

Neal glanced at the object through the plastic and said, "Looks like some kind of a small drill."

"It's a pin chuck, with the drill bit still attached. No doubt our lab will confirm that the tool was used to drill a hole into the canister of Alexa Weller's inhaler." He looked Neal in the eye when he said, "And it was found in your suitcase."

For a few seconds the congressman was speechless, but he recovered fast and stated, "I'm being framed. The thing certainly does not belong to me."

"When was the last time you looked inside your suitcase?"

Angry now, Neal shot back, "I had no reason to look inside! As I told you, I unpacked as soon as I was assigned my room, stored the empty bag in the closet, and never gave it another thought."

There was no comment from Detective Kuwada, and it took all of Neal's self-control to keep his voice civil when he said, "Someone planted that - - whatever you called it - - with the drill bit attached in my room. You won't find evidence that I used that tool, let alone a motive. I had no reason to kill Alexa."

The detective asked, "Who broke off the relationship, you or Ms. Weller?"

"She did. But that was many years ago. You can't possibly allege that I held a grudge strong enough to kill her. That's insane!"

"Sometimes these things run deep," said the detective. And he added, "There may be another motive we don't know about yet. Ms. Weller seems to have had a knack for making enemies."

The detective made a sudden move and knocked down the tissue box on the end table. He bent down to retrieve it and groaned, "Ouch, my back."

Neal quickly came to his rescue and picked up the box, setting it back on its place on the table.

"Thanks! My back acts up whenever I make a wrong move." Then he asked, "Who occupies the rooms on either side next to yours?"

"I don't know. Oh wait, I take that back. The Triests must have a room next to mine, I saw Beatrice Triest step out onto the balcony the other day. I don't know who has the one on the other side."

Detective Kuwada concluded with, "I believe I've already cautioned you about not leaving the island," and he glanced in the direction of his subordinates, asking, "Do either of you have any questions for Mr. Victor?"

"I do," said the female in uniform. "How and where did you meet the victim?"

"At law school. Like I've already stated, it was a long time ago."

Left to themselves, the law enforcers summarized the interrogation. Detective Kuwada said, "So what did you think of Neal Victor?"

The male officer said, "I watched him closely when you told him about finding the pin chuck and drill bit in his suitcase, and his astonishment seemed genuine."

"I paid keen attention too, and agree. He had either no idea that the tool was there, or else he's a damn good actor. I also judge him to be a smart man, and can't imagine why he didn't get rid of the evidence, if he is the guilty party."

"So you think he was framed?"

"Either that, or the killer placed the murder weapon in the next best room he could find with its owner gone, after doing the deed. At this point, though, I'd like to keep an open mind and not disregard Neal Victor as a suspect."

Not without humor, his subordinate asked, "How's your back?"

"Oh, you caught on to that. I wiped the tissue box after Mrs. Triest was done with it, so the only finger prints on it belong to Neal Victor. I doubt that it will do us any good, though; the man is intelligent. Should he be our culprit, I bet his prints will not be on the pin chuck nor the drill bit."

"He was honest about admitting that it was the lady who broke up the relationship," said the female officer.

"True," Detective Kuwada agreed, "but he knew that with a little digging, we could find that out for ourselves."

Then he said, "I also have a question for you. Why did you inquire where and when Mr. Victor met the victim?"

"I felt it was a coincidence that both Kurt Nobel and Neal Victor had dated the victim." She grinned and stated, "We all know how suspicious you are of coincidences, detective! So I figured that maybe the three knew each other socially and she played one for the other. But that idea doesn't fit, since Neal Victor and Alexa Weller already knew each other in law school. It stands to reason that getting engaged to Mr. Nobel happened later."

"Correct. It doesn't fit, but good thinking on your part. In any given case, I allow one coincidence. This had better be the only one we're dealing with."

CHAPTER 28

The guests resumed their leisure activities. Some went snorkeling, others explored the tropical island, but most hung around the pool area. Kurt did not think it was a good idea to go for a dive while the authorities were still on the premises. He told Detective Kuwada that he could be found on the third floor, if needed, either on the putting green, the gym, or his office.

Barbie and Hope, clad in bikinis and covered in sunblock, sunned themselves in the hammocks near the landing. They had brought books along to read, but neither could concentrate on the stories. Hope shut hers, closed her eyes, and gently made her hammock swing from side to side.

After a while she said, "This is so relaxing, I may even fall asleep."

"How can you relax with murder going on around us?" her friend exclaimed.

"Don't exaggerate. One person got killed."

"I'm afraid this may only be the beginning," said Barbie, and there was dread in her voice.

"Now you're being silly! What happened is unfortunate, but Alexa obviously made one enemy too many."

"It doesn't bother you that we have a murderer on the Isle of Ease?"

"Of course it bothers me, but there's nothing we can do about it. We're stuck here until Detective Kuwada lets us leave, so we might as well enjoy the rest of the vacation."

Barbie looked off into the distance and saw a cruise ship appear on the horizon, most likely on its way to Hawaii, and longed to be on it to get away from the isle.

Aloud, she said, "I'm scared. Remember the hermit's warning?"

Hope cried out, "I can't believe you're taking that crazy old man seriously! There is nothing to worry about. As I said, too bad about Alexa, but the rest of us are safe. It's not like there's a serial killer on the loose."

Barbie kept silent and Hope tried to convince her again by saying, "None of us are in danger, and soon the police will arrest the guilty person. And don't even speculate on who that might be; you'd only get yourself into another panicky state." That said, she buried her head in her book, thinking the subject was closed.

Seconds later, Barbie said, "Kurt is edgy too and not his normal assertive self. He said to me at lunch that events at the Isle of Ease had all of a sudden taken a dark turn, and that he was powerless."

"That's understandable. There's been a murder here, and I'm sure he feels helpless at the moment and regrets having invited Alexa in the first place. Also, he's used to being the head honcho. It can't be easy for him to have Detective Kuwada calling the shots."

"What if the police can't solve the crime by the end of the week, or even worse, if they can't solve it at all? Are we going to be prisoners here forever?"

"You are such a drama queen! Snap out of it already. Detective Kuwada is sharp; he'll figure it out. And if by chance he hasn't made an arrest by Friday, I'm positive that he won't be able to legally hold us on the island any longer."

CHAPTER 29

In the den, Detective Kuwada interviewed the domestic employees. There was not much to learn from Emilio, the gardener; Chris, the pool maintenance person; or Rosa, the housekeeper's helper. None of these folks had known Alexa Weller prior to coming to the island, nor had they been aware that she suffered from asthma. Even since her arrival here, they had had minimal contact with the woman.

The cook, Hermina Tovar, walked into what had become the interrogation room, trying to put a grave expression on her jolly face, without much success. It was simply against her happy-go-lucky nature. She was 56, plump, and there was not a single grey strand in her thick, naturally black hair. She greeted Detective Kuwada, nodded to his two subordinates, and took her seat.

The detective started with, "I understand that you are Kurt Nobel's cook. What kind of cooking do you do?"

She grinned and said, "I graduated from a chef's college and can create anything one's heart desires, from French cuisine to unassuming American steak and potatoes, or anything in between." She spoke without an accent, being second generation. Her parents had emigrated from Venezuela.

He remarked, "Your French dip was delicious, by the way. I can imagine that everyone enjoys your cooking."

"Including me! Don't ever trust a skinny chef," she said and winked at him.

The detective said, "It must be a challenge to cook for so many people here."

"I'm used to it. Mr. Nobel frequently entertains guests at his place in Beverly Hills."

"How long have you been his chef?"

"Let me think. He hired me when my youngest graduated from high school. That was seven years ago."

"So you knew Alexa Weller when she was engaged to your employer?"

"Yes, sir. I sure did."

"What did you think of her?"

Hermina said, "The woman was clever and entertaining, I give her that."

"But?"

"She was what I'd call a 'cold fish.'"

"Did you know that she suffered from asthma?"

"Sure. Everybody knew."

He took a moment to reflect on what else he could bring up, and then said, "One last question. When was the last time you saw Ms. Weller?"

Hermina replied, "She came to the kitchen an hour or two before her husband found her dead. Ignoring me, she went over to Domenica, asking for something to drink. Domenica offered to bring the fruit punch up to her room, but she was impatient, as usual, and carried it out of the kitchen herself.

CHAPTER 30

Domenica Cortes was on her way over to the den and thought, first I had to worry about being killed in a plane crash, and now I'm involved in a murder investigation. Where will it all end? She made a pit stop to the bathroom. Being nervous always made her have the urge to pee.

She felt a bit self-conscious at the beginning of the interview when Detective Kuwada cautioned her that one of the officers was recording their talk, and she also realized that the other was taking notes. But she soon switched back to her normal, competent self, ignoring the two officers and focusing on Detective Kuwada, who made her feel at ease, asking general questions about her duties as housekeeper.

He said, "Ms. Cortes, I understand that this is no longer a hotel, but do you take care of the guests' bedrooms?"

"If you mean, do I do the daily dusting, run a vacuum cleaner, and scrub the bathrooms, the answer is no. Señor Nobel said that wasn't necessary until the guests leave on Friday. But I do bring fresh towels for bath and pool use every day, and also make up the beds if they are still unmade."

"Do the guests usually make their own beds?"

"Some do and some don't." Domenica replied, not about to tell who did and who didn't.

"I understand that you work for Mr. Nobel on the Mainland."

She gave him a blank look and said, "What mainland?"

"Sorry, we Hawaiians call the rest of the United States simply 'the Mainland.'"

"Oh, I see. Yes, I work for him at home. I'm the live-in housekeeper at Señor Nobel's Beverly Hills house in California."

"I presume for many years?"

"A long time. Ever since he divorced his first wife."

"So you knew Alexa Weller when she was engaged to your boss?"

"Absolutely. Her last name was different then, of course."

Detective Kuwada inquired, "Did you like her?"

"No," was Domenica's curt answer.

"Was she mean to you?"

The housekeeper looked intently at the blank TV screen behind the detective's back, uncertain how to reply.

After a long pause, she said, "It had nothing to do with me. She was not mean or nice, just ignored me. That didn't matter. As a servant, I'm used to that. I hated what she did to Señor Nobel. Dumping him right before the wedding was spiteful. It took him a long time to get over it."

"Did you know Ms. Weller suffered from asthma?"

She nodded and said, "I saw her having an attack once at the Beverly Hills home. It was scary to watch. But she recovered fast, as soon as she used the rescue inhaler."

Before the detective continued the interview, Domenica said, "On Monday, when we first learned about what happened, I thought that Alexa didn't get to her inhaler in time or that it was broken. Today, you told us that she was murdered. How can that be? Didn't she die of an asthma attack?"

Detective Kuwada explained, "We don't have the autopsy report yet, but it looks like she died indeed from an attack. However, we found that her inhaler had been tampered with. That is why we are conducting a homicide investigation."

He cleared his throat and said, "When I talked with Ms. Tovar, the cook, she mentioned that Alexa Weller came to the kitchen on the afternoon of her death, asking for something to drink. As per Ms. Tovar, you took care of her request."

"That's right. She wanted fruit punch. I filled her a glass from the punchbowl and offered to bring it up to her room, but she preferred to carry it herself."

"It seems then that you were the last person to see her alive."

Offended, Domenica declared, "I didn't mess around with her inhaler!"

"I'm not suggesting that you did." And to soothe her, he continued, "This is important. I wonder if you can help me out with the layout of the guest bedrooms. I understand that they are all on the second floor. I've obviously been to the Wellers' room, but don't know in what order the others are occupied. If you can give me an idea of all the rooms on that floor, and the people who currently stay in them, that would be of great use to me. Start from the spiral staircase and the rooms facing south toward the pool and the ocean."

She thought about it for a couple of seconds, closed her eyes to visualize it, and then said, "Starting next to the stairs and facing south is Mr. and Mrs. Triest's room, next comes the gentleman who is by himself - - I forgot his name."

"Neal Victor?"

"Yes, him. Next to Mr. Victor's room is the elevator, and on its other side is Mr. and Mrs. Weller's room - - I mean, only Mr. Weller's now. Then comes little Evie's small room which connects to the room of Mr. Nobel's sister. Then there is the room belonging to the young woman Hope, and next to hers is a spare room. That is all for the rooms facing south."

She briefly looked up, then closed her eyes again and continued, "On the north side, facing inland and starting by the stairs again, are first two unoccupied rooms, the elevator, and next to it, Mr. & Mrs. Ross's room. Then the guestroom occupied by Mr. & Mrs. Simonian. Next is the laundry room and adjacent to it the room with linen closets and lots of other storage."

He complimented, "You were thorough and precise. Thank you. That information helps with our investigation."

Pleased, she now dared to ask the question that had been on her mind since lunch time. "What did the officer find when searching the politician's room? I keep forgetting his name."

"You mean Neal Victor?"

She nodded.

"What makes you think there *was* something to find in his room?"

She stated, "There had to be. You talked to him a second time."

Detective Kuwada hesitated for a second but then decided that, at this point, there was no harm in telling her and replied, "We found a pin chuck and drill bit." Then he thanked her and ended the interview.

After the housekeeper left, one of his officers said, "That woman is sharp."

"And keeps her eyes wide open, unless she's concentrating," Detective Kuwada remarked with a chuckle. Then he asked his note taker, "Did you jot down the guestroom occupancies in the right order?"

"I did better than that," he replied. "I drew a plan."

"Excellent!"

There was nothing more for Detective Kuwada and his team to do on the island that day than pack up their gear, tell Kurt Nobel that they'd be back, stressing again that no one was to leave the place, and take the helicopter back to Hawaii.

Domenica walked toward the separate structure behind the mansion to check on her own room. She didn't like the fact that the officer had gone through her things; he might have left them in a mess.

Her mind lingered on the interview that had just taken place. She had no idea what a pin chuck was, but what did a drill have to do with killing Alexa? She suddenly muttered, "*Madre de Dios!* He must have drilled a hole into her inhaler."

To her pleasant surprise, she found not a thing out of place in her room.

CHAPTER 31

By Wednesday morning, people on the Isle of Ease made an effort to be optimistic and get their "fun in the sun" back on track. Some achieved it to a degree, and others struggled with the concept.

Barbie didn't feel like going down to breakfast and had hers brought up to her room on the third floor. Kurt came back to kiss her good-morning and said, "I'm taking Rafi out on the yacht for a scuba dive."

"Is that permitted? Remember Detective Kuwada's orders not to leave the island."

"I've promised Rafi a dive off the boat and mean to keep my word. Besides, I consider the waters around the Isle of Ease as part of the island and therefore belonging to me."

Barbie didn't think that was true, but knew better than to argue with him and said, "Have fun, then."

"What are you up to this morning?" he asked.

"Don't know yet," she said, "maybe I'll go back to bed."

Two doors down from the master bedroom suite, Max was working out in the gym again. Not because he wanted to stay in shape, but rather to get away from everyone. He couldn't stand the way people avoided looking him in the eye, or what was even worse, the pitying glances when they did.

While steadily pedaling on the stationary bicycle, he thought, did I make the right impression on the detective? I was hardly in control when he dropped in on me yesterday. And isn't the husband always suspect number one? Then his mind drifted to immediate pressing matters. So far, he hadn't had the courage to call Alexa's folks or let anyone else know about her death. And obviously, he had to make arrangements, even though her body was still stretched out on some coroner's table in Honolulu. He shivered, and then pedaled at high speed, trying to banish that picture from his mind.

Most other guests resumed activities of snorkeling, swimming in the ocean, or hanging around the pool area.

CHAPTER 32

Kim was aware that the last 48 hours had left a tremendous impact on her daughter. She could be temporarily distracted by playing computer games or swimming in the pool, but what had happened had left an emotional burden on her eight-year-old. Even though Evie hardly knew Alexa, she seemed to have admired her. It had been hard enough to soothe her anxiety when they thought that the woman had died from natural causes, but now it got more difficult to answer the child's endless questions.

She'd ask things like, "Mommy, how come the policeman said somebody killed her? Didn't she have an asthma attack?" And, "Why would anybody do such a thing? She was cool." Or, "Mommy, is there going to be a funeral? Do we have to go to it?" Kim tried to satisfy her curiosity by answering truthfully, but with as little detail as possible.

Kurt had invited her and Neal on a dive off the yacht he was doing with Rafi today, but they had both declined. She didn't know Neal's reason for passing it up, but hers was clear. Leaving Evie with strangers at this point was not an option. Her child needed her right now. So she suggested they take a nature walk.

"Are we gonna see wild animals?" Evie asked.

"I doubt it," Kim replied, knowing that there would not be much food for wildlife on such a small stretch of land. "But I bet we'll hear birds and maybe even see some if we're real quiet."

Neal asked whether he might join them. Kim could not think of an excuse why not, yet was a bit apprehensive. True, she liked the man, but the authorities must have had good reason to interrogate him a second time.

He sensed her hesitation and said, "I'd like to talk with you and vindicate myself."

She smiled and said, "Sure, you're welcome to come along."

They walked along the same trail which Barbie and Hope had explored on Sunday. When they started off, the temperature was a comfortable 80 degrees and sunny, with a nice little breeze. Evie tended to run a few paces ahead of her mom and Neal, then waited for them to catch up to point out wonders of nature. For instance, she wanted to know what the five-foot-tall plants with lance-shaped leaves and blue-purple flower clusters were called. Kim told her that she thought they were Blue Ginger.

When they came upon a gorgeous, red, fragrant, flower in full bloom growing on a vine right next to their path, her mom explained, "That's a Perfumed Passion Flower. It is butterfly friendly, meaning that caterpillars feed on its leaves."

Evie rushed toward it and said, "May I pick it, Mommy?"

"That's up to you, Sweetie. If you do, the flower is going to wilt in a few days, but if you leave it alone, other people coming along the trail can enjoy its beauty."

Evie chose the latter and dashed ahead to do more exploring.

Neal thought, she must be a terrific teacher, having more to offer her students than grammar. Her botanical knowledge aside, she also seems to be a great mother.

Aloud he said, "Well put!"

Kim asked, "Do you have kids?"

He replied, "My wife had a couple of miscarriages and then we had a stillborn infant. We were about to try again, when she was diagnosed with pancreatic cancer."

"That is so sad. I meant to tell you I was sorry for your loss, but never found the right moment."

"I wasn't looking for sympathy," he said, embarrassed. Then he braved the subject that had been upmost on his mind and said, "Part of the reason I asked to come along on this walk is because I need to set something straight. First off, what have you heard through the grapevine about me? I mean, concerning what the authorities found in my room."

She replied, "Nobody said anything, at least not to me, but I assume they must have found something incriminating, or Detective Kuwada wouldn't have questioned you a second time."

"Yes, they did. Apparently, the killer drilled a hole into Alexa's inhaler, and the tool he or she used showed up in my suitcase during the officer's room search."

Kim said, "I see. The medication escaped, leaving her inhaler empty. And when she activated the pump during her attack, instead of getting relief, nothing happened and she was destined to die."

"Evidently. But did you hear what I said?"

"You mean the bit about finding the evidence in your bag? You were obviously framed. Only a moron would keep the murder weapon in his possession."

"I'm relieved that you've got it right and can only hope Detective Kuwada sees it that way too."

She asked, "Now that we've got that out of the way, what was the other reason you wanted to come along on our walk?"

He grinned and said, "That one's simple. I like your company."

Evie had joined them halfway through their talk, overhearing part of it. She asked, "What's an inhaler?"

Kim answered, "It's how people with asthma get their medication so that they can breathe."

"Does it come in a bottle, like coughing syrup?"

"No, it's a device they take into their mouths to inhale medication."

"What's it look like?"

"That's hard to describe. There's a mouthpiece and a pump."

"Does it sort of look like a whistle?"

Neal said, "You're right, it sort of does."

Kim wondered where her child might have seen a rescue inhaler and was about to ask, but with her curiosity satisfied for the moment, Evie scurried off again.

They trekked close to the empty vacation houses when rain clouds appeared, and moments later, they got caught in a sudden tropical downpour. One of the dwellings had a bamboo-covered patio area, where they quickly sought refuge. While they waited out the storm, Kim suggested singing. None of them had good voices, but Evie got a kick out of the lyrics from campfire favorites. Then they played, "I Spy," and soon the rain stopped as swiftly as it had started.

As they continued their walk, the old recluse came into sight. He stood on a small mound, shaking his fist as they passed by.

"Hello there!" Neal greeted.

The old man did not respond but gave them a venomous stare and then disappeared.

Kim said, "That must be the hermit Kurt told me about."

"What's a hermit?" asked Evie.

"A loner who prefers nature to people," her mom replied.

"Why is he angry at us?"

"He believes the island belongs to him and sees us as intruders."

"But Uncle Kurt owns it, right?"

"True. Uncle Kurt bought the Isle of Ease, but that man was here first and resents it."

All three were hungry and looked forward to lunch when they returned to the mansion.

CHAPTER 33

After serving the guests their midday meal and helping Hermina put the kitchen back in order, Domenica and Rosa went over to their favorite spot to enjoy their own picnic lunch. On their very first day on the island, they had discovered the secluded bench beneath the blooming peppertree, halfway between the eastside of the mansion and the ocean. Since then, the two had spent a good part of their free time relaxing in the shade of that tree. They had no idea that it was the blossoms of that same tree that had triggered Alexa's asthma attack.

Finished eating, Domenica looked up at the pretty white flower clusters above them and said, "It is so peaceful here. Hard to believe what wickedness has taken place."

Rosa reached into her bag, pulled out her latest project and started crocheting. She nodded and said, "I can't get it out of my mind either." She was able to work on the baby blanket for her newest grandchild with hardly a glance at her fingers, the crochet hook, or the yarn.

Scanning the landscape in the direction of the ocean, she noticed that Mr. Nobel's yacht was anchored at the landing and the hammocks fastened to palm trees were swinging in the gentle breeze. Two wetsuits hung to dry next to the shed at the water's edge. "That reminds me," she said, "I've been worried about something."

"What about?"

"Remember when the detective talked to us all in the dining room?"

"Of course, I remember. Get to the point, Rosa!"

"He told us that if we'd seen anything unusual to tell him about it."

"What did you see?"

"It may not mean anything and is probably okay, but I did see someone come out of the gentleman's room yesterday morning."

"What are you talking about? What gentleman?"

"I think he's a congressman."

By now Domenica had his name down pat and said, "Neal Victor?"

"Yes, him."

"You saw someone come out of his room. So what? The person may have paid him a friendly visit, for all you know."

"That's just it. Mr. Victor wasn't there."

Domenica thought, the trouble with Rosa is that she can't tell a straightforward story. And language is no excuse, we're talking in Spanish.

Aloud she said, "Tell me what you saw, step by step."

Rosa halted her crocheting while trying to verbalize her thoughts and stated, "Yesterday morning, I was delivering fresh towels to the guests, and even though I knew that most were having breakfast in the dining room, I still knocked at every door before entering."

Domenica rolled her eyes, thinking, I asked for it by saying "step by step," but did not interrupt her friend who continued, "When I was about to knock on Mr. Victor's door, someone else came out of it and said something to me, but I didn't understand, because of the loud noise the helicopter made, bringing the detective back. Anyhow, like I said, Mr. Victor was not in his room, and when I went out on his balcony to see if things needed straightening, I found an empty glass, but the gentleman was not there either.

"I didn't think much of it, until later, when the detective said we should tell him about things that we considered odd. When he interviewed me, I was scared and didn't say anything about it. I still don't know whether to tell him or not. I don't want to get somebody innocent into trouble. Maybe I should talk to the person first. There could be a simple explanation. I'm gonna call Carlos tonight. He'll tell me what to do."

Domenica thought, how typical of Rosa, seeking her husband's advice. A widow for a long time, she was self-reliant and did not understand her friend's dependency. She said, "That's up to you, but maybe you shouldn't let Carlos know about what happened here just yet. He may want you to come home straight away."

"You're right," said Rosa. "He'd fly off the handle!" And she promptly made the decision to go straight to the source.

Domenica asked, "So who is this person you saw coming out of Mr. Victor's room?"

At that moment, Mike and Beatrice walked by in swimming attire, obviously planning to go for a dip in the ocean.

"I'll tell you later," Rosa whispered, wondering how much of their conversation the pair had overheard, and returned to crocheting at high speed.

CHAPTER 34

Later that afternoon, Rosa was humming a tune while folding towels in the laundry room. She congratulated herself for having made the right choice. A good thing she had not told the detective what she saw, or it would have made her look like a fool. She was glad to have gone straight to the person and now that she knew the harmless explanation, it was a great relief, like a big burden was lifted off her shoulders.

And Domenica was right that telling Carlos what had happened on the island would be a mistake. He had not wanted her to come here in the first place, and she'd had to use great skills of persuasion until he was finally okay with it. Letting him know that a lady got herself killed here would make him worry and probably angry too. Her Carlos had a temper.

What's more, she started to believe that the police were wrong and the lady had accidentally died from her asthma attack, just like it was first assumed. Of course, that was still tragic, but not as scary as knowing someone had deliberately killed her. She felt a bit remorseful for not being the least bit sad, but then, she hadn't known the woman at all.

Rosa was still humming the cheery melody to herself when she heard the door behind her being opened.

She turned around and said, "Oh! Did you mean to give me something to launder earlier?"

The person entered, and pulling the door close replied, "Not exactly. I came to do this."

With a swift move, and before she registered what was happening, the individual wrapped a doubled-up piece of heavy-duty leader fishing line around her neck and yanked it tight.

Rosa opened her mouth to scream, but the sound that escaped her was only a barely audible gurgle. She struggled for a couple of heartbeats, while the person pulled the leader tighter and tighter, but didn't stand a chance. The strangulation was over within seconds and then the killer let her slide to the ground and tied a knot in the leader line.

The murderer opened the door a crack, listened intently for footsteps or voices in the hallway and, hearing none, sneaked out of the laundry room, then nonchalantly walked on.

CHAPTER 35

After their lunch together, Domenica took advantage of the fact that most guests were occupied outdoors and applied herself to straightening and feather-dusting the rooms on the ground floor, while Rosa went to do laundry. Domenica was done with the two bathrooms, the living and dining rooms, den, and game room, when she heard the sound of piano playing coming from the music room. That must be Señor Nobel's young wife working in there, she thought. I'd better not disturb her.

She decided to give Rosa a hand in the laundry room. While taking the stairs up to the second floor, she realized that her friend had put off telling her who she had seen coming out of Neal Victor's room. After their conversation was interrupted by the pair who passed by, Rosa never got back to the subject. Domenica did not think what Rosa had seen was important. There could be many valid reasons why someone went into that particular guestroom while its owner wasn't there. Still, she was curious and wanted her friend to tell her who the person was.

She opened the door to the laundry room, saying, "You forgot to - - -"

An ear-piercing scream escaped her as she looked down at Rosa's lifeless body and dull eyes, staring at her from a grotesque face, bluish in color, with a narrow plastic rope around her neck.

Sick to her stomach, Domenica turned on her heels and ran back to the hallway, shouting, "Help! Somebody help!"

Kate, who had changed out of her bathing suit into a sundress, stuck her head out her guestroom door and saw Domenica - - now beyond words or screaming - - pointing to the open door of the laundry room. Kate walked in that direction and entered, with Domenica close behind her. Rosa was not a pretty sight, and Kate had a hard time keeping her lunch down. Then she took a couple of deep breaths and was able to pull herself together. She bent down to Rosa's body and felt for a pulse. As expected, there was none.

She turned to Domenica and said, "I know you've had a great shock, but you have to take charge now. Go find Mr. Nobel and tell him to contact the authorities."

As soon as Domenica went in search of her employer, Kate shut the door to the laundry room, quickly went to her own room next door to get a chair and her tablet, and then stationed herself by the entrance of what she considered the crime scene. Having done plenty of research about police procedures, she knew that nothing should be touched in that room until the authorities got there, so she would guard the door until they'd arrive.

When Kurt hurried along, wanting to see what had happened for himself, she couldn't refuse him entry. After all, she was only a guest and it was his house, but she warned him not to touch the victim.

He took one look and erupted in anger.

"What the hell! Is one dead body not enough?" he yelled as he passed her by on the threshold. By the time he reached the elevator, he had calmed down enough to call the authorities.

Kate's own nerves somewhat restored, she opened her tablet and added the event of the day to her journal.

CHAPTER 36

Kurt entered the music room where Barbie sat at the piano, composing her own song. She had the melody down pat and was working on the lyrics, repeating them several times, trying out different versions. She had not heard him come in but suddenly sensed his presence and turned her head.

Seeing the distressed expression on his face, she asked, "What's the matter?"

"I have more bad news," he said, "Rosa was strangled to death."

Barbie's reaction was intent and took Kurt by surprise. She first turned white as a ghost and then grabbed both his arms and pleaded, "I'm scared! Take me away from this island."

As Kurt held her close, he felt her trembling and said, "What happened is tragic, but really Barbie, you hardly knew the woman."

"Alexa and Rosa are only the beginning. We are all doomed. How many more people will have to get killed before you realize it? "

Kurt said, "Now you're being dramatic. It stands to reason that Rosa knew something about Alexa's murder and was silenced. I've already called the authorities, and I'm sure Detective Kuwada and his men will get here at any moment. I have every confidence that he'll solve the two crimes."

As if Barbie had not heard a word he said, she exclaimed, "Let's get out of this place! There's a curse on the Isle of Ease." And she told him about the encounter she and Hope had had with the hermit on the north shore.

Kurt had a sudden urge to laugh but suppressed it, bearing in mind their grave situation.

He said, "That old man is off his rocker. His threat can't be taken seriously and has nothing to do with what's going on here. I have known ever since I built the hotel on the island that he resents having what he considers trespassers, around. I thought he was harmless, but now I'm not so sure, since he's able to get you all worked up." And he added, "Any talk about a curse and us being doomed is pure superstition."

Again, Barbie did not react to his comment and said, "Can we at least leave Friday, like planned?"

"I aim to keep everyone's flights back home as scheduled. No matter what, Detective Kuwada can't keep our guests here indefinitely."

That reassured her a bit. Having lost all desire to work on her new song, she gathered the sheets of music and closed the piano lid.

She stood up and asked, "How did it happen?"

"What?"

"About Rosa. How and where?"

"I told you, she was strangled. As to where, Domenica found her in the laundry room."

"How do you know she was strangled?"

Kurt took a deep breath, recalling the disturbing sight, and said, "I saw her. She had leader fishing line tied around her neck."

Barbie shivered and cried out, "How horrible!"

The loud sound of a helicopter approaching, carrying Detective Kuwada and his team to the island once again, made it impossible for any further conversation.

CHAPTER 37

The coroner put Rosa's demise at approximately two to two-and-a-half hours prior to his examination of her body, and his preliminary findings were cause of death by strangulation. Once again, the helicopter pilot transported another dead victim from the Isle of Ease to Honolulu. The coroner and his assistants accompanied the corpse, leaving Detective Kuwada and his team in charge on the island.

After they had finished with the crime scene, the detective informed Max Weller that the autopsy on Alexa was completed and that her body would be released shortly. As expected, the autopsy revealed that she had suffocated by an obstruction that blocked the airflow to her lungs, due to an acute asthma attack. She could have been saved with medication from her rescue inhaler, but as evidenced, the hole in the inhaler made that an impossibility.

Next, the systematic questioning of the suspects took place all over again. This time Detective Kuwada saw no need to keep the group of people in one room, since no search took place. He informed them that it was okay to keep to their activities, as long as they stayed either in the mansion or on the grounds nearby until questioned.

He started with Domenica. There was a huge change in the housekeeper since her interview of the previous day. Gone was the competent attitude and no-nonsense demeanor. The woman looked physically ill, pale and swollen-eyed from crying.

Detective Kuwada said, "I realize you've had a great shock. I understand that it was you who found your co-worker in the laundry room."

"She was not my co-worker," Domenica stressed, "she was my friend!"

"But also Mr. Nobel's employee?"

"No, I brought her here. It's all my fault. If I hadn't, she'd still be alive." Domenica had a hard time keeping from falling to pieces.

The detective realized this and steered her in a different direction. He said, "Tell me what you did today, starting from lunch time until you found your friend."

She complied. "After we served lunch to the guests, Rosa and I had our own lunch at our favorite bench under the peppertree."

"Did Rosa seem in good spirits?"

"Overall, yes, but she saw something yesterday that worried her. She asked my advice what to do about it, and stupid me, I didn't realize how important a thing it was. I should have told her to call you people. Instead, she must have decided to go to the killer."

"You mean, she may have tried her hand at blackmail?"

There was fury in her swollen eyes as she shouted, "Don't you dare say such a thing about Rosa! She was a good woman."

"I take that back," the detective said. "Why do you think she went, like you say, to the killer?"

"She didn't know the person was Alexa's killer. I'm sure she thought that whoever it was had an innocent reason for going into that room, and so she went to ask that person."

Detective Kuwada was at a loss as to what the housekeeper meant and said, "You need to tell us what you learned from Rosa." And so she related the entire conversation that took place while the two women ate their picnic lunch.

Detective Kuwada paid keen attention and then asked, "Rosa didn't mention who she saw coming out of Neal Victor's room?"

"No. We were interrupted. She was going to tell me later but never did."

"Interrupted by what?"

"Guests were walking by us."

"Who?"

"It was Mr. and Mrs. Triest."

"Did you see anyone else on your lunch break?"

"Hope De Luca and Mrs. Simonian were on their way to go snorkeling."

"Close enough to hear your conversation?"

"Sure. The writer lady even wished us 'buen provecho.'"

"Anyone else?"

She had to think about it and then said, "When we first got there, Emilio was blowing the fallen blossoms away from the bench with his blower, making a racket."

The note taker cleared his throat and made Domenica jump. She had forgotten that the two assistants were there.

Detective Kuwada continued with the interview, "What did you two ladies do after lunch?"

"Rosa went to take care of laundry and I straightened up and dusted the rooms on the ground floor."

"At what time was that?"

"About 1:30."

"What was it when you went to the laundry room?"

"About half an hour later," she replied. "It must have been close to two o'clock."

"By the way, what made you decide to go there?"

"I was gonna help Rosa with the wash and I was also curious. She hadn't told me - - -"

Domenica broke off as the horrid scene of finding her friend stretched out on the floor with that ghastly thing tied around her neck and those unseeing, staring eyes, flashed back into her mind.

The detective said, "I know this is painful, but we need to know. Did you touch the victim?"

"No, I couldn't. She was too grotesque and I knew she was dead."

"What did you do then?"

"I ran out to the hallway and called for help. Mrs. Simonian came out of her room next door and sort of took over."

"Meaning?"

"She told me to calm down and go look for Señor Nobel while she made sure nobody would go into the laundry room. I ran up the flight of stairs, which was faster than waiting for the elevator, and found him in his putting green room."

"What made you look for him there?"

"I knew that he'd been back from scuba diving much earlier, since Rosa and I saw his yacht anchored at the landing when we ate our lunch. I figured he must be on the third floor, since I hadn't seen him anywhere on the ground floor when doing the dusting. I first pounded on his bedroom door and got no response. Then I realized that the door to the putting green stood wide open, and I found him practicing his putting."

For a few moments there was perfect silence in the den. With the interview coming to an end, Detective Kuwada mulled over the important facts he had learned from this witness; the recording officer was waiting for a sign from him to turn off the machine; the other had caught up with taking notes; and Domenica tried hard to get the disturbing picture of Rosa out of her mind.

She suddenly cried out, "I have to tell Rosa's husband. *Madre de Dios,* help me!"

Detective Kuwada thanked her and let her go. To his subordinates he stated, "If the housekeeper was accurate with her times, Rosa's homicide was committed between 1:30 and 2:00 p.m. That would fit with the coroner's initial finding. We got here at 3:50 p.m., and he said he estimated that the victim had died two to two-and-a-half hours before that time."

His male assistant said, "Looks like Domenica Cortes happened upon the crime scene just minutes after the victim was strangled."

"That seems to be the case."

"So we'll check people's alibis from 1:30 to 2:00."

The female officer said, "I have a question unrelated to Ms. Cortes's interview. The murder weapon used for strangulation was heavy duty fishing line, correct?"

Detective Kuwada, who was a fisherman on his off-duty days, answered, "A leader was used, to be exact. The leader is attached to the main fishing line for extra strength when going after big fish."

Then he stated, "Now we had better interview Kurt Nobel. I expect he has his nose bent out of shape because I didn't talk to him first."

"You can't blame him; this is his domain and you've taken control of it," she remarked with a smirk.

CHAPTER 38

Kurt and Sidney were shooting pool in the game room. Kurt was losing. With his mind stuck on the two murders on his island, it was difficult to concentrate on the game. While his opponent was making one perfect shot after another, he thought back to his talk with Barbie in the music room, where he had assured her that Detective Kuwada would let them all leave the island soon. Now he wasn't so sure.

When one of the detective's subordinates came to fetch him, he was eager to interrupt the game and told Sidney, "I'll catch you later."

In the den, the first thing he asked Detective Kuwada was, "Have you made any progress with your investigation in finding Alexa's killer? I can't keep my guests here beyond their scheduled return home on Friday."

"We're working on it, and plan to keep at it, 24/7," the detective replied. "At this moment, though, I'd like to concentrate on today's homicide." And with barely a smile he said, "I apologize for not having talked to you first. You stated in your call to us that Ms. Cortes found the body, so I wanted to interview her right away, while the experience was fresh on her mind."

"Makes sense," Kurt commented.

Detective Kuwada said, "I need to ask everyone's whereabouts of today. Please give me an account of yours, let's say, from when you left the dining room after lunch, until you notified us of the new tragedy."

Kurt replied, "I took Rafi on a dive off my yacht this morning, and we didn't eat our lunch in the dining room. Hermina packed us some food, which we ate on board. I'm aware that you ordered us to stay put on the island but believe that the surrounding waters belong to the Isle of Ease."

The detective did not think that was so, but he let it slide and said, "At what time did you come back from your boat trip?"

"I can't be precise, but it was around 12:30 in the afternoon."

"Continue, please."

"We returned our diving equipment to the shed and hung our wetsuits to dry. Then I went to shower, and I assume Rafi did the same. Once cleaned up, I had planned to suggest to Barbie that the two of us go for a walk - - she loves walks and hikes - - but I heard her hard at work in the music room and decided that our walk could wait. Instead, I went up to the third floor again and practiced putting on my indoor putting green. I was only on hole number 6 when Domenica burst into the room with the horrible news about Rosa."

"What time was that?"

"I didn't look at my watch but had checked the time minutes earlier as I stood outside the music room. It was 1:45 then."

"What happened after the housekeeper alerted you?"

"I wanted to see for myself and rushed to the laundry room, where Kate Simonian stood guard at the door but stepped aside when she saw me coming. It was a ghastly scene." He swallowed twice, as the disturbing picture re-entered his mind.

The detective gave him time to recover and then asked, "Did you touch her?"

"No, sir. I knew better than to do that."

"Good. And then you called us?"

"Yes, right away."

The detective checked his records and nodded. "Your call came in at 2:05."

Then he asked, "Did you come across any guests either on your way to or inside your mansion, after returning from your diving trip?"

"Rafi walked with me to the house. We took the elevator up; he went out on the second floor, and I continued on to my room on the third. We saw people in the pool area while passing, but I didn't pay attention who they were. Inside, I heard folks playing in the game room but didn't go over to say hi. Taking a shower was all I had on my mind at that point."

"Thank you for the precise account of your movements. And now to something else. Since you saw the dead woman, you must be aware what she was strangled with."

Kurt stated, "A leader was used."

"Ah, we're talking one fisherman to another," the detective said, with a grin. "Where would one find leader line on the premises?"

"I keep a supply of it in the shed." And then it seemed to hit him. He bellowed, "The nerve of the killer, using my leader!"

Detective Kuwada said, "We will have to inspect the shed."

"No problem."

"Now to something else again. I don't understand your relationship to the strangled victim. Domenica Cortes said that Rosa was her friend and not your employee. Did you not pay her for her services?"

"Of course I paid her, but she was not my domestic employee at home. I only hired her for this week on the island to help Domenica. It is true that Rosa was Domenica's friend. In fact, when I asked Domenica to come along to the Isle of Ease, I left it up to her to bring as much extra help as required. She assured me that her friend Rosa was all she needed."

The detective thought, no wonder the housekeeper feels that what happened is her fault for bringing the woman to the island in the first place.

He could not think of anything else to ask and was about to end the interview when Kurt pointed a finger at him and said, "You'd better solve this matter quickly. As I already told you, my guests are ready to leave Friday. They took this week off from their busy lives but need to get back to their commitments. Also, I'd like to remind you that Easter is coming up on Sunday."

It was clear to Detective Kuwada that he had been given an order. Unintimidated, he replied, "I can't make you any promises, Mr. Nobel, but rest assured, this case is our top priority."

CHAPTER 39

Kate Simonian was called next to the den. She sat down in the "hot seat," and before Detective Kuwada had a chance for questioning, said, "No doubt you want to know my movements of today." She opened her tablet with the current journal entry and handed it to him.

"You came prepared," the detective remarked. And he read aloud from the tablet, so that the text was getting recorded:

"Wednesday, April 12:

We had a bit of a tropical rain mid-morning, which was refreshing. I happened to be swimming in the pool at the time, which made it rather fun. After all, wet is wet! The downpour lasted but a few minutes. I was thinking of Rafi on his scuba dive and wondered if he would even realize that it was raining above.

At lunch, I overheard the two young women, Barbie and Hope, debating what to do next. Hope tried to convince her friend that snorkeling was fun and not dangerous in the least. Barbie wanted no part of it, stressing that no matter what the other claimed, just putting on the mask would make her feel claustrophobic, let alone swimming below the surface. Besides, she had this idea of a new song floating around in her head. Hope stated, "I guess I'll have to go snorkeling alone then." I decided to butt in at that point, telling Hope that I'd be happy to join her when she was ready to go snorkeling, which we did a while later.

We explored lots of fish and other sea creatures, but regretfully, I don't know what type they were. Once home, I plan to buy a book on underwater wildlife so that I can familiarize myself with what I saw. Hope is an interesting young woman. On our walk to and from the ocean, we both deliberately stayed away from discussing Alexa's murder. She told me about her longtime friendship with Barbie, as well as her studies and on-campus college life. She also questioned me about my writing and admitted reading mystery novels in her spare time. I may have made a new fan!

Little did we know that real-life tragedy was about to hit us again. I had just finished dressing after a quick shower when I heard a cry for help coming from the hallway. It was Domenica, who was clearly in shock and pointing to the laundry room. Describing what I saw there as disturbing would be a gross understatement. The horrific sight of Rosa strangled made sweat pearls form on my forehead, and I had to fight down the urge to vomit. I pulled myself together, told Domenica to fetch Kurt, and then stationed myself in front of the crime scene room so nobody would mess with it until the authorities arrived. Naturally, Kurt needed to take in the scene for himself before calling the police.

At the moment, I'm still sitting in front of the laundry room, trying not to picture what lies behind its door."

Detective Kuwada took a moment to reflect on what he had read. Then he said, "We thank you again for guarding the entrance to the laundry room. As I told you already when we arrived on the scene, good thinking on your part. Thank you also for letting me read today's entry in your journal. I still have a few questions, though. Did you touch the victim?"

"Yes. I made myself feel for her pulse, even though I knew there wouldn't be any. I thought that I owed it to her to make sure."

He nodded. "Did you happen to check the time when the housekeeper called for help?"

"Not then, but I did look at my wristwatch as I sat down in front of the laundry room door. It was two o'clock."

"Did you see your husband after you came back from snorkeling?"

"No, he and Kurt apparently came back from scuba diving earlier." She smiled and added, "There were signs in the bathroom that Rafi had taken a shower, and he also left me a note."

"May I ask the content of the note?"

"Oh, it was nothing intriguing. He wrote that I could find him in the game room, is all. Needless to mention, I never got the chance to meet him there, since as you know, I was occupied elsewhere."

Then he said, "In your journal, you mention that you deliberately didn't discuss Alexa Weller's murder with Hope. Whose suggestion was that?"

"I've lost you, detective."

"What I mean is, was it you or Hope who decided that it was best not to talk about it?"

"Neither. We simply did not bring up the subject. It seemed a silent agreement."

"Did you see other people on your way to and from snorkeling in the ocean?"

Kate thought about it for a moment and then said, "Kim and little Evie were entering the pool area as Hope and I passed by on our way to the shed. Some other people were already there; I believe it was Neal Victor and also the Ross couple. Domenica and Rosa were sitting on a bench in the shade of a tree full of blossoms, having their lunch. As we came out of the shed donning snorkeling gear, Mike and Beatrice Triest walked down to the water, obviously going for a swim."

She continued, "On our way back, I was exhausted. Hope is a strong swimmer and I barely could catch up with her in the water. She is also a fast walker. On the return trek to the mansion, she only slowed down when she realized that I was panting. There were some people in the pool area, but at that point I wasn't paying attention to who was there, concentrating solely on catching my breath."

Detective Kuwada's next question was strictly routine, something he needed to ask each suspect, whether or not he already knew the answer. He asked, "Did you know Rosa before coming to the island?"

"No, sir."

"How about the housekeeper, did you know her beforehand?"

"Definitely. Domenica has been Kurt's live-in housekeeper for many years. He's got a real gem there." And she added, "If you're going to ask about his other domestic staff on the Isle of Ease, I've met Hermina the cook once or twice at his Beverly Hills estate, and I've also seen Emilio there from a distance. I've never met the pool maintenance young man - - whose name I don't know - - before coming here."

There was something nagging at the back of Detective Kuwada's mind that made him reluctant to end the interview with Kate Simonian. He felt there was an important question he needed to ask her. After a long silence, realizing that she and his two officers were waiting, he could not put his finger on what was bothering him and had no choice but to dismiss her.

As soon as she was out the door, he remarked, "There goes a woman with her eyes wide open."

"Unless she's concentrating on catching her breath," his male assistant said.

CHAPTER 40

The following is what Detective Kuwada and his subordinates learned from the rest of the suspects regarding their whereabouts during the crucial time between 1:30 p.m. and 2:00 p.m.:

Max Weller said that he was in his room, calling his in-laws and making funeral arrangements. Barbie stated that she had been in the music room the entire time, composing a new song. Kim assured him that she and Evie never left the swimming pool area during that time. Neal Victor said he was with them, swimming and playing with Evie in the pool until 1:45, at which time he went to his room. The Ross couple stayed in the pool area until 1:40, when they too went to their room to freshen up. The Triests were getting back from their swim in the ocean at approximately the same time and also headed up to their guestroom. After her snorkeling adventure with Kate, Hope went to her room to shower, and Rafi claimed to have been in the game room, playing Donkey Kong and pinball machines.

As for the domestics, Emilio was working on the estate grounds; the cook was in her room in the separate structure, taking a nap; and Chris, the pool guy, was also napping, although in one of the hammocks near the landing, during that critical time.

It was already early evening when the last interview came to an end. Detective Kuwada and his team inspected the shed and took the leader line they found there with them as evidence. The lab people would compare the leader with the piece that was used in the strangulation of Rosa, to see if it was a match.

There was nothing left for Detective Kuwada and his subordinates to investigate on the millionaire's island that day. He told Kurt Nobel that he'd stay in touch, and they boarded the chopper for Honolulu.

CHAPTER 41

The two tragedies had left their mark on Evie. Kim thought that it had been hard enough keeping up a positive attitude around her child after Alexa's death, and when it had been determined a homicide, the task was even more of a challenge. Now, after what happened to Rosa, putting a neutral spin on matters was no longer an option. People were on edge, and having had the authorities back interrogating everyone again made it impossible to keep Evie in the dark.

Instead of reading a story before bedtime, which she normally looked forward to doing, the girl asked numerous disturbing questions. Kim had always been frank with her and was not about to change that now, regardless of how hard it was.

Evie asked, "Are Mrs. Weller and Rosa in heaven?"

"I hope so, Sweetie."

"Did the same person kill both of them?"

"I think so."

"Why?"

"Rosa must have seen or heard something incriminating to that person."

"What does 'incriminating' mean?"

"It means give him or her away."

After a pause she asked, "May I tell Daddy about Mrs. Weller and Rosa when he picks me up on the weekend after Easter?"

"Of course, you may. And now, let's not talk about it anymore. Why don't you read a little before bedtime?" And so she did, and Kim hoped that was the end of that type of questioning.

But later, when tucking Evie in, she asked, "Mommy, are we all going to be killed if we've seen something incriminating?"

Kim took her child into her arms and replied, "Of course not! None of us have seen any such thing. And certainly, none of us are going to be killed."

The Triests were getting ready for bed, and when Mike came out of the bathroom, Beatrice was near tears again and said, "I wish you hadn't talked me into coming to this place. I had bad vibes about it and was right. Two women got killed, and God only knows who will be next!"

"Don't get overly dramatic," he said, "I don't like what happened either, but there won't be any more murders. I guarantee it."

She gave him an angry look and stated, "You guaranteed that Alexa would decline the Nobels' invitation and not show up at all. Instead, she got herself murdered."

He admitted, "I was wrong about that, but I'm not wrong now. There could only be one reason why Rosa was strangled, namely that she knew or witnessed something that would implicate Alexa's killer."

Beatrice could no longer hold back the tears and cried, "I'm scared. There is a ruthless criminal in our midst! Doesn't that bother you?"

"Of course it does, but there isn't much we can do about it."

"We can leave. Let's arrange for a helicopter or boat first thing tomorrow morning."

Mike replied, "You heard the detective. Nobody is allowed off the island."

"What's he going to do if we take off, arrest us?"

"No, but there may be legal consequences."

Stubborn, Beatrice insisted, "He can't keep us here against our will indefinitely."

"True, but I bet he and his team are close to solving the murders." And he put his arm protectively around her shoulders and said, "In the meantime, try to enjoy the rest of our stay."

Beatrice was lying awake deep into the night while her husband slept next to her. She asked herself, how can he sleep like nothing had happened? Suddenly scared, she got up and shut their door to the balcony, which they had always left open during the night.

CHAPTER 42

At his headquarters in Honolulu, Detective Kuwada was still at work late at night, going over his officers' notes and recordings from the previous and that day's interviews. He felt that it was essential to learn what type of person the first victim was in order to solve her murder. Everyone agreed that Alexa had been above average in looks, but besides that fact, the suspects' opinions of the woman varied. He mulled over each person's statement.

Her husband had said, "We had our differences, but I loved her." Kurt Nobel's account was, "She had a tendency to mock people." Kim Frederique admitted that Alexa had not been on her "favorite person" list. Sidney Ross stated having been attracted to the stunning woman but not liking her. The petite, elegant Heather Ross's comment was, "The woman had a lovely figure and clothes to die for." In Rafi Simonian's words, "She was hot, but I don't think she had soul." His wife Kate Simonian found the victim witty and amusing.

Neal Victor made it known that part of the reason he accepted the Nobels' invitation to the island was because he was curious about Alexa, whom he had dated years ago. Beatrice Triest had hated Alexa and thought she was to blame for the verdict in the malpractice suit regarding her son's death. Mike Triest also hated her for the same reason but in addition blamed her for what Alexa's part in the trial had done to his wife.

Domenica did not like Alexa because of how she had treated her employer. In Domenica's words, "Dumping him right before the wedding was spiteful." Hermina Tovar had called Alexa clever and entertaining, but a "cold fish." Barbie Nobel had been evasive in her interview when asked how she felt about her husband's ex-fiancée. Although she had only met Alexa Weller for the first time on the island, she must have formed an opinion of her. The fact that she was reluctant to voice it spoke volumes. Rosa, Emilio, and Chris did not volunteer their judgement of Alexa. Whether they had not made up their minds about her, or didn't want to say, was unclear to the detective.

He stared at the information in front of him for a long time. There had to be a clue in all that was said, but he just did not see it. He further mused, drilling that hole into the canister of the inhaler could have been done at any time when Alexa was not in her room, from when the guests first arrived on Saturday until Monday afternoon, before her husband found her dead. There was most likely an opportunity for anyone on that island to sneak into the unattended room during that time.

Of course, if Max Weller was the killer, the hole could have been drilled at any other time since last November. Maybe it was more productive to concentrate on the second murder. There was only a half-hour time window in which that homicide could have been committed.

Detective Kuwada went over the interviews of the current day. Having done so, he burst out aloud, "Hell, everyone was taking a shower, was on the way to their guestrooms or was at some other place without any witnesses during the crucial time between 1:30 and 2:00 p.m.! Any one of these people could have taken a few minutes time out to sneak up on Rosa in the laundry room, strangle her, and gone back to their room or respective activity."

This case is driving me insane, he thought, and called it a night.

CHAPTER 43

Evie woke up from a nightmare, screaming. Kim rushed over to her child's room, turned on the light, and then held the frightened girl in her arms.

She assured her, "It's okay, Sweetie. You had a bad dream."

Evie trembled and between sobs stammered, "The man chased me, wanting to kill me."

"Hush, Sweetie, it was just a dream." But then realizing her daughter needed to talk in order to calm down, she asked, "What man?"

"The man we saw on our walk."

"I see. Your dream was about the hermit."

"Yes, he chased me and got closer and closer, and I couldn't move - - he turned into other people and they held me down - - trying to kill me with a whistle that grew bigger and bigger - -"she broke off and winced in terror.

Kim held her tight, saying, "It's okay now. Your nightmare is over. You are safe."

Max Weller, in his guestroom next to Evie's, had another restless night. The shriek that had escaped his mother-in-law when he told her of Alexa's death was still ringing in his ear. Alexa had been his in-laws' only child and their pride and joy. For now, he only told them that she'd had a fatal asthma attack, which was hard enough for them to accept. He hadn't had the guts to reveal to them that she was murdered.

Unable to fall asleep, Max heard Evie's ear-piercing screams next door. He got up, quickly donned his robe, and went out to the balcony. Seeing the light on in Evie's room, he stuck his head in, asking, "Are you all right?"

Kim replied, "Everything is fine. Evie just had a bad dream, but thanks for asking."

"Good to know," he said, and vanished again.

Kim asked her child, "You *are* fine now. Right?"

Evie nodded. "But can I cuddle up in bed with you?"

"Sure you may, Sweetie."

Hand in hand, they walked through the connecting door separating their two rooms. Once safe and sound in the queen-size bed, feeling her mother's closeness, Evie fell back asleep within seconds. Kim was not that lucky. When she heard her daughter's regular breathing, she sneaked out of bed and went to close both bedroom doors to the balcony. To hell with taking in tropical fresh air; feeling safe was more important. Until the two murders were solved and Detective Kuwada made an arrest, she could not trust anyone.

She lay awake for what seemed like hours. The events on the island had had a tremendous impact on her daughter. The horrible nightmare and all those disturbing questions she had asked earlier were proof. The faster they could leave, the better. The idea of having to endure another dreadful day of not knowing who the killer was made her shudder. No matter what, by Friday they'd better have the detective's permission to go home, or she would make a big stink. The emotional well-being of her child was at stake.

CHAPTER 44

Early on Thursday morning, Detective Kuwada was back at his desk. He was pleasantly surprised when someone from the lab department handed him the report concerning the leader. He had asked for a rush order and now acknowledged that the lab technician had taken his request seriously. The report covered technical jargon as to the exact materials contained in the leader, but its bottom line was that the leader taken from the shed matched the one used in Rosa's strangulation. There was an enlarged photo attached, showing an exact match. The detective had expected this result but was pleased to have proof of it now.

He thought, but where does that leave me with the investigation? Anyone from that entire household at the Isle of Ease could have gone to the shed and equipped himself or herself with leader line. It didn't even need to have been yesterday. The culprit could have planned ahead. According to Domenica Cortes's account of the chat with her friend under the peppertree, Rosa had seen someone - - supposedly the murderer - - come out of Neal Victor's room on Tuesday morning, just about the time we landed on the island. All our suspects, at one time or another since Tuesday morning, had had good reason to be inside, or near the shed.

And another fact which had struck him when he first saw that hole in the inhaler crept back into his mind. Alexa could have had the fatal asthma attack at any time after her week on the Isle of Ease. There was no way of knowing when and where she would have it. After all, it had been over four months since her last one. Unless it was her husband, the guilty person must have wished that she would have her next asthma episode, and therefore die, elsewhere.

Continuing his musing, he told himself, whether I like it or not, I have to speculate as to motive. It stands to reason that Rosa's murder was a direct result of witnessing something incriminating about Alexa's homicide. She needed to be silenced. So I must concentrate on possible motives for the first murder. Alexa Weller was disliked by many and seemed to have a knack for making enemies. But was she despised enough for someone to take action to end her life?

The detective took each person into consideration, starting with her husband. Max Weller may well have been the only person on the island who could have financially gained by her death. He admitted that he and his wife had had their differences but claimed to have loved her. What differences? Detective Kuwada wondered. Had they been on the brink of divorce? Did he have a life insurance policy on her? Was the wealthy pharmaceutical mogul suddenly in financial difficulties? He made a note of looking into all that.

Kurt Nobel's invitation to treat his former fiancée to a week on his island to celebrate his recent marriage to Barbie was odd indeed. In fact, having invited all his other unlikely guests was also bizarre. But then, millionaires - -

and he could well be a billionaire - - were known to be eccentric. He chuckled to himself when thinking, it would have even been weirder had he also invited his first wife. As for being dumped by Alexa six years ago, it would take a stretch of the imagination to consider that fact a motive for murder.

Barbie, as Nobel's new bride, could hardly have been happy sharing their place in the sun with his former fiancée. Even if she had not a shred of cattiness in her, it would be natural for her to resent the other's presence. Enough to want her dead, though?

The detective could not come up with a motive for Kim Frederique, even though she acknowledged not having liked Alexa. Her only tie to the victim had been through her brother's engagement, dating back over six years. There was always the possibility that there existed a severe grievance on her part toward Ms. Weller, unknown to the detective. He skipped over Evie; considering the child as the culprit was ludicrous.

Had Kurt Nobel or Neal Victor been the homicide victim on the island, he would have looked at either as one of the main suspects. The two men hated each other, ever since running for the same seat in congress to represent California. Their highly publicized campaign had been vicious on both sides, to the point that even the detective, who normally was not interested in Mainland politics, took notice.

As it stood, with Ms. Weller being the victim, it was harder to believe Neal Victor as the villain. He had dated her when they had both attended law school, way over a decade ago. If he had harbored a grudge against her, the vendetta would have cooled off by now. He may have an ulterior motive, as yet undiscovered. After all, he is also a lawyer and will presumably go back to practicing law when his term is over. The man is intelligent. If he is the villain, leaving the pin chuck and drill bit in his suitcase doesn't make sense, unless he didn't have time to get rid of the evidence. Also, when considering Neal Victor as the guilty party, Rosa's murder would have to be looked at from a different perspective.

The Triests seem to have a strong motive, the detective thought. Blaming the defense attorney for what they considered an unjust verdict in the malpractice suit concerning their son's death had been a big chip on their shoulders. He could not picture Beatrice Triest planning and executing the thing with the pin chuck and drill bit, though. And her husband did not strike him as the handyman type either.

Detective Kuwada scratched his head and went to the next person on his mental list. He was at a loss to arrive at a motive for Sidney Ross. The only thing that crossed his mind was that the man may have made a pass at the victim, and she had threatened to file a sexual harassment suit. It was far-fetched, but one never knew with middle-aged men. The same thing could apply to Rafi Simonian. As far as he could see, neither of their wives had any reason to kill Alexa Weller.

Of the guests, that left Hope De Luca, who had been a total stranger to the victim. As was established when they discovered the hole in the canister of the inhaler and found the pin chuck with the drill bit, Alexa Weller's murder had to have been planned since February. A spontaneous decision to kill her once on the island did logically not apply.

The two domestic employees who knew the victim before this week were Domenica Cortes and Hermina Tovar. Domenica admitted to having hated her. Her hatred stemmed from a strong loyalty to her boss. It seemed that, contrary to Kurt Nobel, who wanted to show that he had no more hard feelings against his former fiancée, his housekeeper was not ready to forgive her that easily. Hermina Tovar, the cook, did not seem to have liked the victim either, but her aversion was far less strong than Domenica's.

It was established that all other domestic help, alive or dead - - the gardener, the pool maintenance guy, and Rosa - - did not know Alexa Weller beforehand. There was always the possibility that someone lied, and that there was a connection after all.

Disgusted with himself for not being any further in his investigation than before starting his deliberating, he closed his eyes and let his mind go blank. He suddenly remembered fragments of interview conversations, realizing there was a contradiction. Kurt Nobel had said that there seemed to be no animosity toward Alexa Weller among his guests. Yet, the detective recalled reading in Kate Simonian's journal that she'd sensed bad vibes going out in the direction of Alexa on their boat ride over. Granted, according to his information, the Nobels had arrived a day earlier and were not on that boat, but he assumed the hostility toward the victim would have continued. It could be that Kurt Nobel was unaware of it, and Kate Simonian, being a sharp-eyed woman, was more perceptive.

He tried to remember more text from her journal. What was it that had struck him as important? Too bad that there didn't exist a recording of the portion of the woman's journal taken when he was alone with her during the first interview. He could kick himself for not having read it aloud.

He looked away from his desk and noticed an officer walking into the department, then thinking better of it - - obviously having forgotten something - - and watched him running out the door again. At that moment it hit him. It was about the child, running from one room to another, out on the mansion's balcony!

He leafed through his records, found the number he was looking for, and dialed it.

CHAPTER 45

Kate watched Rafi shave and said, "I dread going down to breakfast. Bet you it'll be an encore of last night's eerie silence at dinner. People are scared of their own shadow. They seem to be on their guard, watching each other with suspicion. Shall I go down to the kitchen and have Hermina fix us something that I can bring back to our room?"

Rafi said, "Don't ask me anything while I'm shaving, or I'll cut myself."

"Sorry!" she said. And stepping out of the bathroom, she reconsidered and decided that her suggestion was not a good idea, as she was liable to run into Domenica in the kitchen. The poor woman was pitiful to watch, full of grief over losing her friend.

Kate's phone went off. She looked at the time. It was shortly after eight o'clock. She quickly calculated that Los Angeles being three hours ahead made it 11:00 at home. Let it not be one of the boys calling with bad news, she thought. Not recognizing the caller's number, she sighed with relief.

"Hello, Mrs. Simonian? Detective Kuwada here. I hope I'm not intruding on you too early?"

"No problem, we're up."

"I have a question. It concerns something I read in your journal during your first interview. Please refresh my memory on what you observed on the balcony of the mansion, concerning Kim Frederique's daughter. Try to be as specific as you can."

Rafi came out of the bathroom, asking, "Something wrong at home?"

She shook her head and motioned him to be quiet. To the detective she said, "Oh, that was just something I found amusing at the time. Is it important to your investigation?"

"It may be."

"Let me think back." Reflecting on it, she stated, "It was on Sunday, shortly before lunch and after I came back from my first snorkeling experience. I left the snorkeling equipment in the shed and started walking toward the castle - - I mean the mansion. I saw little Evie coming onto the balcony from her room - - at least I assumed it was from hers - - and then she vanished into the adjacent guestroom. As I got closer to the mansion, she appeared again on the balcony and ran back into what I believed was her own bedroom. That's all I saw. At the time I imagined that the child was bored and must have found a way to amuse herself, by inspecting some other guestroom."

Detective Kuwada asked, "Do you know who occupies that other room?"

"I don't. My husband and I have a room facing inland. I'm unfamiliar in what exact order the rooms facing front are assigned to the guests."

"From your viewpoint when approaching the building, did Evie go to the adjacent guestroom east or west of her own room?"

"West," Kate replied, without hesitation.

Then he asked, "In your estimation, about how much time elapsed from when you saw the girl enter that other guestroom until she reappeared on the balcony, running back into her own room?"

"Not long. Four minutes or so. I guess it took me maybe three minutes to walk up from the shed, and then I stopped to talk to people in the pool area for another minute."

"Thank you! You've been specific, which helps me a lot," said the detective, and ended the call.

Then he consulted the plan of the guestroom layout his subordinate had drawn during Domenica Cortes's interview. He whistled to himself, thinking, just what I expected: The guestroom adjacent west of Evie's was at that time occupied by Alexa and Max Weller.

CHAPTER 46

When Kim's phone rang, Evie was still asleep, exhausted from her ordeal of the night. In order not to wake her, Kim walked through the connecting door to the adjacent room before answering it. Hearing Detective Kuwada's voice, she quickly closed the door behind her, and the two had a lengthy conversation. When he first informed her that he needed to interview Evie, Kim was outraged.

She said, "I forbid it. Whatever you have to discuss with my child will have to go through me."

He insisted, "It is necessary that I talk to Evie directly. At this point, what she may know is essential to my investigation. Of course, her being a minor, you'll be present at the interview."

Kim protested, "Evie is already traumatized enough. I won't let you upset her even more."

"I'm aware that the homicides must be disturbing to the child. I have small kids of my own and know how to deal with the situation in a sensitive manner."

"You don't understand! Evie admired Alexa and had a hard time dealing with her death to begin with. When you people determined that Alexa was murdered, Evie had tons of questions."

Surprised, the detective said, "I didn't realize your daughter knew the victim before coming to the island."

"She didn't. Evie was only two years old when my brother's engagement to Alexa ended, so she didn't remember her. For some strange reason, Evie took a liking to the woman when meeting her here."

"Interesting."

Kim continued, "The thing with Alexa affected Evie deeply, and what happened to Rosa added to her anxiety. Last night, she was tormented by nightmares."

"I'm sorry to hear that, but the fact remains that I need to talk with the child. I believe it is best to conduct the interview here, at our Honolulu headquarters."

Kim remembered numerous movie scenes where suspects were dragged into interrogation rooms. She pictured her daughter in a drab, dark, uninviting cubbyhole of a room, sitting on a hard, uncomfortable chair, with only a small, bare table between her and the detective, bombarding her with questions.

He heard the dread in her voice as she asked, "In an interrogation room?"

"Nothing as intimidating as that," he assured her. "It can be held in my office, without my team, just with Evie, you, and me."

The idea of escaping the gloomy Isle of Ease atmosphere came as a pleasant surprise to Kim. Still, she had to ask, "Why do you want to see us in Honolulu and not here?"

There was a pause in the line while the detective searched for words that would be the least alarming for what needed to be said. He settled on, "If I'm correct in my estimation, Evie may be in danger after talking with me."

"Oh great!" Kim shouted. And worrying that she may have woken Evie, she swiftly opened the connecting door to her bedroom and peeked inside, but her child was still lost to the world.

Detective Kuwada went on, "If I'm on the right track, she may even be in danger period, whether she talks with me or not. So here is what I suggest: If my hunch is right, you and Evie should not return to the island after the interview. And should I be wrong, there would be no particular danger to her and you would be free to return to it."

Kim stated, "There is a killer among us here. No matter what, if we're leaving, we're not coming back."

"Good thinking! I will arrange for a chopper to pick you up this morning. One more thing, Ms. Frederique. Don't advertise to the folks on the Isle of Ease that you and Evie are leaving."

As soon as they ended the call, Kim started packing. Evie suddenly stood next to her in the walk-in closet, asking, "Why are you putting stuff into the suitcase already? We're not leaving until tomorrow, right?"

Kim said, "Good morning, Sweetie. There has been a change of plans. How about you and I go on a helicopter ride and then spend our last night of the trip in a hotel in Honolulu?"

"A helicopter ride? Cool! Right now?"

"First we pack, then go down to breakfast, and then wait for the helicopter to pick us up."

Evie asked, "What's there to do in Honolulu?"

"I was just getting to that," her mom replied. "Detective Kuwada wants to talk with you."

"Why?"

"He called a little while ago and said he needed your help with his investigation."

"Me? I can't help."

"I know, but he thinks that you can."

"How?"

Kim bent down in front of her child until eye level with her and said, "Listen, Sweetie, if you've heard or seen anything suspicious, the detective needs to know. But first, you must tell me about it right now."

"I don't know anything, Mommy," Evie replied.

CHAPTER 47

Neal sat next to Kim and her daughter at breakfast. Evie asked him, "Are you coming with us on the helicopter ride to Honolulu?"

When he gave Kim a puzzled gaze, she had no choice but to explain the situation, despite Detective Kuwada's warning not to advertise their leaving the island.

Making light of the situation, he turned to Evie and said, "How exciting for you! First you get to ride in a chopper, and then you'll be interviewed at police headquarters in Honolulu, like a real important person. I wish I could come along, but I wasn't invited." He added, "But I'm looking forward to seeing you tomorrow on our flight back home."

Kim was aware that Evie had taken a liking to Neal. The fact came as a surprise. Ever since the messy divorce of her parents, Evie refused to have anything to do with any adult male figure in her life. She seemed to come back from weekends spent with her father more confused and anxious rather than reassured and secure. The only exception was her uncle Kurt, who spoiled her, and in return she adored him. Not that Kim had done much dating, being gun-shy herself.

She suddenly realized that Neal was studying her, and when he saw that Evie was preoccupied with eating her pancakes, he lowered his voice and said, "Are you okay with her being questioned by the authorities?"

"No, but I don't seem to have a choice in the matter."

He touched her hand lightly and asked, "After all this is over, may I see you?"

"You're asking me out on a date?"

"Not now, but yes, once we're home and have recovered from the ordeal on the island."

"Let's wait and see," she replied cautiously.

She noticed her brother and Barbie making their way out of the dining room, and said to Evie, "Stay put. I'll be right back."

Kim rushed after them and caught up by the elevator. Addressing Kurt she said, "I need to have a word with you."

"Sure, shoot."

"Not here, let's talk in the den."

The elevator door opened and Barbie stepped into it, saying to her husband, "See you upstairs."

As expected, there was nobody in the den early in the morning. They settled themselves on upholstered chairs and Kurt asked, "So what's the secret you couldn't openly discuss in the foyer?"

"No secret. It's just that Detective Kuwada didn't want me to broadcast it, but I feel that you have the right to know that Evie and I are leaving the Isle of Ease this morning."

"What do you mean?"

Kim explained the status quo. He heard her out and then exploded, "Why the devil does Kuwada want to interview Evie? She's only eight years old, for crying out loud!"

"He seems to think that she knows something incriminating to someone about the murders."

"Like what?"

"I have no idea."

"That's ludicrous! If that were true, she would have told you or me or most likely both of us about it."

Kim said, "Unless she doesn't understand that what she either saw, heard, or knows has something to do with the killings."

"I guess that's possible." And he got mad again and said, "Then why the hell doesn't he talk to Evie here, like he did with everyone else? Why haul her to Honolulu on a chopper?"

Kim replied, "The detective thinks she may not be safe here." And she declared, "The good part is that Evie is looking forward to the helicopter ride."

"I can understand that, but getting interrogated at the police station is going to be traumatic for her, no doubt." Picturing it got him all worked up, and he shouted, "Detective Kuwada is dragging his feet with these murders. He should have solved them by now. Instead, he's asking for the help of a little girl! How absurd is that?"

"I'll be there with her during the interview. Rest assured, I'm not going to let him intimidate my Evie."

Kurt calmed down and said, "Unless Evie insists on a helicopter ride back, I'll come pick you up in the yacht when you're done."

"We're not coming back to the island and plan on staying in Honolulu overnight, since we're flying home tomorrow."

"Yeah, that makes sense. What hotel have you booked?"

"I don't have a reservation; I'll play it by ear."

"Leave it to me. I'll reserve you a suite at the Hilton."

"Thanks!" She got to her feet, and hugging her brother, said, "Thank you for having had Evie and me as your guests. We had a great time for the first two days. I'm sad for what happened afterwards and am sorry that it ruined yours and Barbie's joyful celebration."

As Kim walked back to the dining room, she heard the sound of the helicopter approaching.

Seeing mother and daughter lifted off the island by the authorities' chopper did not improve the mood of the guests who remained. Unanswered questions were being voiced, like, "What did they do?" "Why are they getting special treatment?" "How come they get to leave and we don't?" "What the heck is going on now?" and so forth.

Evie enjoyed the exciting ride, while Kim puzzled over the strange text message she received on her phone.

CHAPTER 48

The helicopter landed on the roof of the headquarters building, and then Kim and Evie were ushered into Detective Kuwada's office, leaving their two suitcases in the hallway. The small room of about sixty square feet was a no frills sort of place, with a white board mounted on one wall and a window on the opposite one. The space in the center was taken up with a large desk, behind which Detective Kuwada sat.

He got up when they entered and offered them seats on the two chairs that had been placed to face him across the desk.

"Thank you for coming," he said, and addressing Evie, inquired, "Did you have a good ride over?"

"It was cool," she replied, still in awe of the adventure.

Then he got to the point and continued, "I believe that you can help us with our investigation concerning what happened on the Isle of Ease. I need to ask you important questions and you must answer them truthfully. Because you are a minor, your mommy can object, if she feels the question is inappropriate. Do you understand?"

Evie nodded and said, "I know what 'inappropriate' means."

"Good. Let's start, then. For the record, I'm taping the conversation, but you need not concern yourself with that."

"I'm gonna be on a video?"

"Just an audio," he replied with a smile, and recorded her name and other relevant data.

Kim interjected, "Before you start, tell us why you think that Evie can help with the investigation."

"Believe me, Ms. Frederique, I have a valid reason, but let's hear Evie's story."

He bent down to Evie again and said, "Do you remember what you did on Sunday, April 9, in the late morning?"

Evie looked at Kim and asked, "Was that when we went snorkeling?"

"No, Sweetie. We went snorkeling after lunch. Detective Kuwada wants to know what you did before that time. Remember, I went scuba diving with Uncle Kurt, Mr. Simonian, and Mr. Victor and left you in the care of Mr. and Mrs. Triest."

"Oh yeah, they were swimming and playing with me in the pool."

The detective took over and inquired, "And then what happened?"

"Nothing. I went up to our rooms to shower."

"What did you do after you showered?"

She averted her eyes and said, "Nothing. Mommy came back soon afterward."

He said, "Evie, look at me: Remember what we agreed on? It is important that you tell the truth and leave nothing out."

Instead of raising her eyes to the detective, she turned to Kim and confessed, "I went into Mrs. Weller's room and tried out her eyeshadows." And her eyes suddenly turned moist as she begged, "I'm sorry, Mommy. I didn't mean to do it, but the colors looked so pretty, I couldn't help it."

"Don't worry about that. Just tell us what happened."

And so Evie stated what she had witnessed through the crack of the Wellers' closet. The way she worded it was that the culprit fiddled with something she had never seen before, which looked like a whistle. She hadn't paid close attention to what he was doing, since it took all her concentration to hold back a sneeze. She just hoped that he would hurry up and be done soon, so that she could leave her hiding place unnoticed.

The detective opened the top drawer of his desk and then reached for two transparent evidence bags. He held the first up to Evie and asked, "Is this what you thought looked like a whistle?"

"Yeah, that's it."

For the recorder's sake he stated, "The witness identified the rescue inhaler."

Then he showed her the other evidence bag and asked, "Are these the tools the person used to work on the inhaler?"

"That's right," Evie said, and he indicated, "The witness identified the pin chuck and drill bit."

And then the detective thought it was time to get to the essence of the interview and asked, "Were you surprised to see the person in that particular room?"

"Yeah, at first. When I heard someone open the door, I thought it would be Mrs. Weller, catching me using her makeup."

"What I mean is, were you astonished to see someone not belonging in that guestroom?"

"No. It's his room too."

Kim could not help herself and butted in, "So it was Mr. Weller you saw tampering with the inhaler?"

Evie stated, "No, it was Uncle Kurt. The house belongs to him, so all the rooms do too."

One could have heard a pin drop in the silence that followed. Kim was shaken to the core; Detective Kuwada's face was expressionless; and Evie hoped that she did not get her uncle into trouble.

Kim, still in shock, suddenly remembered the text message she had received from her brother while on the helicopter ride over. She showed it to the detective. It read:

"If you can, make an excuse of needing to get rid of your luggage and check in at the hotel first. I'll meet you there. If they don't let you, I'll see you at the Hilton after the interview is over. In any event, I'll make it worth your while."

He read it carefully, then turned to Evie and said, "Telling us what you saw in the Wellers' room on Sunday morning was hard for you. You've been honest and helped me a lot. How about a treat of ice cream? One of my officers can take you to the cafeteria in the building, while I have a discussion with your mommy."

Uncertain, Evie looked at Kim who said, "It's okay Sweetie, go ahead."

CHAPTER 49

Kim watched her child leave the room with a female officer. She recovered from the shock enough to ask the detective, "How did you know what Evie witnessed?"

"I didn't know, just had a hunch. Someone saw her out on the balcony, going from her own room to the Wellers', and then staying there for about four minutes. That's a long time to spend in someone's room if just curious to have a look around."

"I don't think the significance of what she saw fully registered with Evie yet, and when it does, it will disturb her deeply. She loves her Uncle Kurt." Kim took a deep breath and added, "I'm having trouble dealing with it myself."

"I am sorry," the detective said and meant it. "Considering the text message from your brother, we need to make immediate plans. Evie and you may be in danger. I suggest that you lodge at a different hotel and let us deal with the situation at the Hilton."

"Meaning you'll arrest him?"

"We can get an arrest warrant, but the testimony of an eight-year-old may not hold up in court for a conviction. I'll try to coax him into a confession."

The idea of Evie having to testify in court sent shivers down Kim's spine.

There was a long pause in their conversation, during which Kim fought an inner battle to either protect her own kin, or seek justice for Alexa and Rosa. Doing the right thing won.

She stated, "There is no way my brother would ever harm Evie. So we'll go to the Hilton as planned. Knowing Kurt, he may be waiting for us there already. I'm sure he wants to buy us off. So you can equip me with a listening device, or whatever you call those things."

Detective Kuwada said, "That is generous but most of all gutsy of you. I may take you up on the offer. We'd be close by, of course, to intervene as soon as there'd be any indication of a threat to you or Evie."

"There won't be; I'm 100% sure of that."

"Okay, then, let's get organized," he said and put his words into action.

When the female officer dropped Evie off at the detective's office minutes later, he and Kim were finished with the preparations.

She called a taxi, then took Evie by the hand, saying, "Let's go have lunch at a nice restaurant and then we'll check in at the hotel," feeling like a traitor.

CHAPTER 50

Kurt ordered his own helicopter and hightailed it to Honolulu. His guests were irate to see him leave, demanding to know what was going on. He left them in the dark. At this point, he couldn't care less about appearances. Barbie, asking to ride along, was harder to appease. He told her that he needed to get Kim and Evie out of a bind in a hurry, and would tell her all about it upon his return.

Now, he sat in the hotel lobby, waiting for his sister and niece. He had been there for a long time and knew that Evie's interview was either taking place at that moment or was already over. Too bad he hadn't been able to prevent it. Having no idea what incriminating knowledge Evie could possibly have, it was hard to know what to do about it. He was surprised that the girl did not come to him with any questions about whatever it was that she had learned. He thought that would have been natural, considering their close relationship. But then, it looked like she hadn't confided in Kim either. Go figure the mind of an eight-year-old, he mused. For the umpteenth time he failed to come up with what his niece's knowledge of the crime could be.

No use to further speculate, he told himself. Evie would soon tell him and then he'd take it from there. No matter what she knew - - or thought she knew - - the testimony of a small child would hardly stand up in a court of law. He was sure that it would never come to a trial at all. He would cut a deal. After all, he was good at it and had millions at his disposal.

His careful plan had worked like a charm and he was not about to let it fall to pieces now. It felt good that, at last, Alexa got what she deserved. Too bad about Rosa, but he had had no choice but to make sure she would never talk. No matter what Evie's evidence turned out to be, he would make sure Kim would bury it.

Realizing that he was hungry, he checked his watch. It was already past noon and since by now Evie's interview with Detective Kuwada must have already taken place, talking business with Kim could wait. He might as well have lunch in the restaurant across the street. He left the lobby and headed there, making sure to obtain a window seat, so he could watch the hotel entrance.

Half an hour later, he saw them getting out of a taxi and then vanishing inside, followed by a porter with their luggage. Kurt decided to give them some extra time to settle into their rooms before making his appearance.

CHAPTER 51

Since they were only staying for the one night, Kim unpacked what they needed for the rest of the day and evening, and their outfits for the plane ride home, leaving everything else in the suitcases. Their suite had a spacious sitting room, equipped with a mini-sofa and a couple of upholstered chairs, coffee table, and refrigerator. The adjacent bedroom was also roomy, furnished with two queen-size beds, nightstands, armoire, dresser, full mirror, and a big-screen TV. The airy bathroom had a walk-in bathtub, separate shower, and double-sinks.

Kim was sure that Kurt had paid for their accommodation, making what she had to do even harder. She was thinking, *Kurt, hurry up, so we can get this over with before I change my mind,* when there was a knock at the door.

Evie hollered, "Who is it?"

"Your Uncle Kurt!"

Surprised, she yelled, full of excitement, "Mommy, Uncle Kurt is here!"

Once inside, he gave them each a big hug, which Evie returned with enthusiasm, while Kim received hers with a heavy heart.

Kim said, "There's water in the fridge, or I can offer you something from the bar."

All three were thirsty and opted for water. Kurt and Evie got comfortable on the sofa and Kim sat down on one of the chairs. Evie asked her uncle, "Why did you come to see us?"

As if it was the most natural thing in the world, he replied, "I need to know what you told Detective Kuwada this morning."

So Evie told her story one more time. Kurt listened carefully, and even though learning that she'd witnessed his crime was news to him, no expression of surprise showed on his face. Once she arrived at the end of her narrative, Evie became sad.

She said, "I hope I didn't get you into trouble, Uncle Kurt."

"Don't worry. If you did, I can fix it."

Then he got up and said, "Come, let's see what movie you'd like to watch while I discuss things with your mommy. When I made the reservation, I told them to make sure to include a kids' selection." And the two walked into the bedroom.

Evie searched through the choices and then exclaimed, "There's Harry Potter. Cool!"

Kurt set her up with the Harry Potter movie, which would keep her happy for a couple of hours, he estimated. More than enough time for talking with Kim. Closing the door to the bedroom, he thought, Evie was the easy part. Dealing with Kim would be the bigger challenge. But then, she was his baby sister and, so far, he had always been able to dominate her.

CHAPTER 52

When Kurt came back into the sitting room and before he even sat down again on the sofa, Kim burst out, "I can't believe you could do such a horrific thing!"

"You don't understand. Alexa had it coming!"

And for the first time in six years, he voiced his anger at the woman who had haunted and taunted him all those years. The words came out slowly, almost in a stutter at first, then faster and faster, leading him into an emotional frenzy.

"Three nights before the wedding - - after lovemaking, no less - - she said, 'I've changed my mind. Let's call off the wedding.' At first I thought she was kidding, and like a fool agreed. Then she gave me that devilish laugh of hers and in her deep voice told me that she was serious. I tried to talk some sense into her, but she didn't budge. When I pointed out that we couldn't give over 300 invited guests such short notice, her damn answer was, 'That's your problem; you've invited most of them.'"

He took a deep breath and continued, "I loved the woman. Dumping me like that for no good reason, as far as I could tell, hurt me deeply. I admit, it also wounded my ego. I knew I would be the laughingstock of the general public and could picture the headline, 'Millionaire left at the altar.' The next day, I went to see her at her office, trying for the last time to change her mind, but it was no use. She laughed at me, and with a mocking expression said, 'Face it, Kurt, it's over. There won't be a wedding, so sue me!' I decided right then and there that I'd find a way to kill her, even if it would take years.

"Barbie had it almost right. She remarked that, deep down, I was still in love with Alexa. It was not love but an obsession. I was possessed by the woman and couldn't snap out of it, no matter how hard I tried. You'd think that with the passing of time, my fixation would fade. Not at all. It became even stronger, like a curse. On the rare occasions when our paths crossed, either socially or professionally, she managed to get me riled up all over again. I couldn't get her taunting face off my mind for months. My hatred grew like a cancer. The only way I could rid myself of being obsessed with Alexa was to eliminate her."

He paused, took a sip of water, and when Kim didn't comment, he went on, "It wasn't easy to find a way to get close enough to Alexa to do the deed. Believe me, I spent years trying to come up with a foolproof plan but failed. During the conversion from hotel to private residence on the Isle of Ease, the idea of a celebration and having an excuse to invite guests came to mind. The more I thought about it, the more I liked the idea. Thanks to Detective Kuwada and his team, you know how it was done."

Kim asked, "How could you be sure Alexa would have an attack on the island?"

"Oh, I had no idea when she would have her next attack. I was hoping that she'd have it at home or somewhere else. If so, I wouldn't have been a suspect at all. But just in case her asthma attack came on the Isle of Ease, I needed to invite some people who would also have an ax to grind with Alexa, should the hole in the inhaler be discovered."

"I see."

"I was betting on the fact that the authorities would think the inhaler malfunctioned and the coroner determined accidental death. I didn't see the need to get rid of the pin chuck and drill bit right away. But then, when I heard the helicopter approaching again early in the morning on the next day, I knew why Detective Kuwada and his team were coming back."

"And you stashed the evidence in Neal's room to frame him," Kim said, getting angrier by the minute.

"I had to think of something in a hurry, having barely enough time to get it and then plant it in his room before meeting the authorities as they climbed out of the chopper. I was hoping that Detective Kuwada didn't notice my being slightly out of breath from running."

She glared at him and said, "So you murdered Alexa because you thought she'd wronged you and you held a grudge. I get that, but by no means condone it. Now tell me, what did poor Rosa do to you to deserve the same fate?"

"I'm sorry about her, but she knew something that incriminated me and needed to be silenced."

"Tell me the Rosa story. I want to hear all of it."

Kurt knew that it was not a good idea to do so but had the urge to tell it anyway, as he was on a roll now.

He stated, "I was worried about Rosa, since she saw me coming out of Neal's room after I dropped the pin chuck and drill bit into his suitcase. Like an idiot, I said the first thing that came to mind, 'Have you seen Neal Victor?' I don't think she heard me, though, because of the helicopter noise. I was hoping that she didn't give it any thought. After all, I'm the owner of the place and have a right to be in anyone's room. Still, I was on pins and needles during Detective Kuwada's interview with Rosa. Since he didn't question me about it later, I was somewhat relieved, but equipped myself with leader line from the shed, in case the woman would put two and two together and become a threat.

"When she came looking for me in the putting green room, stammering and full of apologies, but nevertheless questioning what my business in - - what she called the gentleman's room - - had been, I knew that I needed to act fast, before she told anyone about it, if she hadn't done so already. My first impulse was to hit her over the head with my putter, but of course, I couldn't let her be found on the third floor. So I pacified her for the moment by telling her that Neal Victor had borrowed my phone and I went to his room to get it back."

Kim interrupted, saying, "So why kill her? You could have just left it at that, if the explanation satisfied her."

"No, I couldn't. Sooner or later she would have connected the dots, if not alone, with the help of someone else. I'm sure she wouldn't have kept the knowledge to herself."

He scratched his head and said, "Now where was I? Ah, yes - - when she left, I stuck my head out the door to see if she was taking the stairs or the elevator. I was in luck. She chose to ride down and waited for it. As soon as the elevator door closed behind her, I sprinted to it and listened whether it would stop on the second floor or go all the way down. She got out on the second, so luck was with me again. There was only one room she could possibly be heading for on that floor at that time of the day. The rest was easy. I went to get the piece of leader I had ready in my own room, and surprised her in the laundry room."

He sighed and continued, "During my interview about Rosa's murder, I had to make a time adjustment in my statement to Detective Kuwada. When I stood listening to Barbie's piano playing outside the music room door, the time was not 1:45 in the afternoon, like I told the detective, but in fact only 1:35. The strangulation actually took place at 1:45. It was exactly 2:01 when Domenica came to sound the alarm. I checked, even though I told the detective I didn't know the exact time. The reason for my discrepancy about the time is that nobody would believe I had been practicing putting for almost half an hour."

Kim felt physically ill. During Kurt's entire disclosure, a single thought never left her mind: How could her own brother be a cold-blooded murderer?

He said, "And now that you know it all, let's talk business."

She desperately needed a break from him and said, "Let me check on Evie first."

CHAPTER 53

Evie was mesmerized by the movie she was watching and did not hear or see her mom coming into the bedroom, so Kim sneaked out again. Then she forced herself to go back and face her brother.

Kurt said, "Since I took so long spilling my guts to you, time is running out. Detective Kuwada has most likely arrived at the Isle of Ease with a warrant for my arrest, and is on his return from there now. The man is no dummy and must be figuring out what I'm up to, as we speak."

She said, "There is nothing more to discuss. If you came to bribe us, you're too late. As you well know, Evie told it all to the detective. And even if you had caught up with us before the interview, you couldn't have bought us off."

"Bribe is too strong a word. I prefer calling it a business deal. As far as what Evie told the authorities, I doubt that an eight-year-old's testimony would hold up in a court of law. And without it, Detective Kuwada and his minions have nothing whatsoever on me."

His crooked smile made her flinch as he said, "Here's the deal: You tell the detective that Evie made the whole thing up. Or if you prefer, inform him that she had dreamt it all, and then couldn't distinguish between what was real and what was in her dream. I leave the details up to you. Just make sure he'll believe that the entire episode was a fib the girl conjured up."

"You are disgusting!"

"Hear me out. How does ten million sound? Seven million for you and three million into a trust fund for Evie. I understand university educations cost a fortune nowadays."

Revolted, Kim shook her head.

"You drive a hard bargain, Sis. Okay, let's make it fourteen million; seven each. Or you can divide it any way you like."

Kim shouted, "Get it through your thick skull; Evie and I are not for sale! You can't buy yourself out of a murder conviction, no matter how many millions you're offering."

She was suddenly aware of the open door to the bedroom with Evie standing at its entry. "Why are you yelling, Mommy?" Evie asked.

"Sorry, Sweetie. I got carried away. Uncle Kurt and I were having an argument. Go back to watching Harry Potter."

As soon as the door closed behind her daughter, Kim said, "And don't you dare mention anything of this to Evie. I will not have you corrupt my child."

Kurt shot back, "Have it your way, but you'll regret it. I'll never make the same offer again. Mark my word, there's no way I'll be convicted because of Evie's story alone, and there's no other evidence against me. So I'll go free, whether you take the money or not."

Kim stated, "That's where you're wrong. There will be more evidence!"

He stared at her in utter disbelief, and Kim realized that the truth dawned on him at that very instant.

"You're wired?" he asked, already knowing the answer. She nodded.

"You're doing this to your brother! You sure are a piece of work," he yelled.

All the fight suddenly went out of him. He got up from the sofa and walked over to where Kim sat on the chair, then stood close to her and said loud and clear, "Detective Kuwada, listen to me! I give up. Grant me one wish, though. Don't burst into the hotel room, where my niece can watch me being handcuffed. I'll step out into the hallway and you can arrest me there."

And without another glance at his sister, he walked out the door and out of her life.

EPILOGUE

On a Saturday morning in May, Kim and Neal were out on their first date. It was not your average dinner and a show, but a hike in the San Gabriel Mountains to the Monrovia Canyon Falls. Neal had suggested it, knowing that Kim was as nature-minded as he. He picked her up at her Arcadia home and then drove them to Monrovia Canyon Park where he left his car. They found the trailhead behind the park's Nature Center.

Although it was only a short hike to the fall, it was all uphill, and consequently they talked little. At one point, Falls Trail crossed a creek and they rock-hopped to the other side, where they continued hiking along it amid a lush grove of alders.

The trail came to an end at the Monrovia Canyon Falls. They delighted in listening to the peaceful, soothing sound of the water cascading down the rock face. After exploring the area for a bit, they found the perfect place for their picnic, sitting on boulders below the fall. Neal unloaded his backpack, and they lunched on turkey and Swiss cheese sandwiches, washing them down with Perrier. For dessert, he brought out a mango, which he had cut into small pieces ahead of time.

Having swallowed their last bites, Neal smiled and said, "Now let's talk. How is Evie coping? I half expected that you'd bring her along."

Kim replied, "She wanted to come, but this is one of the weekends that she spends with her dad. As far as coping, she's not doing well emotionally. What happened on the island, and especially her part in it, is leaving its mark on her psyche. I hope and pray that the damage is not permanent. She has nightmares on and off. Needless to say, she still loves her Uncle Kurt and has a hard time accepting the facts."

"Poor kid. Will she have to testify at his trial?"

"Thank God that won't happen! Kurt, in fact, wanted to make sure Evie would not have to be involved and confessed."

"At least that!" Neal commented. "And you, how are *you* holding up?"

She sighed and replied, "I have good days and bad days. I cannot come to terms with the fact that a brother of mine was capable of murder."

"I read someplace that every human being is capable of it, given certain circumstances. Kurt must have had a hatred beyond normal for Alexa to have lasted six years."

"I always knew that Kurt held grudges when someone dared cross him. In Alexa's case, the emotion ran deep. Not only did she have the nerve to defy him, but she mocked and ridiculed him doing it. He felt humiliated to the bone when she ditched him three days before the wedding, leaving him to deal with ceremony cancellations and the embarrassing chore to notify the invited guests at the last minute. It would have been awful for the average person, but for someone with his ego, it was pure hell. From day one, Kurt had a love/hate relationship with Alexa. He had a strong physical attraction for her, but she brought out the worst in him."

They stayed silent while a group of hikers came close by to admire the waterfall. Neal thought, I hope she understands that I don't mean to pry, but she needs to talk about her brother in order to get her peace of mind back.

When the hiking party left, Kim continued, "I feel like a traitor," and she told the part she played in Honolulu, on the day of Kurt's arrest.

As she finished her tale, he looked into her sad face, reached out and held her hand, saying, "Never forget. You did the right thing."

"Yes, but he is my brother and it hurts."

They sat quietly for some time, just holding hands. Kim felt refreshed with sudden strength, coming from his touch.

Then he asked, "How is Barbie doing?"

"I sat next to her on our flight home and she seemed overwhelmed. I haven't seen her since. She'll get over it in due time and I imagine that she'll divorce him. Who knows, the publicity she's getting out of the whole thing may even help her singing career. I can picture her writing a song about it all."

"What's going to happen with all of Kurt's businesses?"

"I don't know and don't care," Kim answered with conviction.

At that moment, Neal knew that his departed wife would approve of Kim. And the woman at his side reflected that a future with him would not be a bad idea. And so they hiked back down the canyon the way they came.

Kim had been right about Barbie. At that very moment, the talented young woman was in the process of composing a new song. Working on the refrain lyrics, this is what she came up with:

> *"Hey Hermit on the north shore track*
> *You may have your island back."*

Stand-Alone Mysteries by Alice Zogg

Accidental Eyewitness
A Bet Turned Deadly

R. A. Huber Mysteries by Alice Zogg

Evil at Shore Haven
Guilty or Not
Murder at the Cubbyhole
Revamp Camp
Final Stop Albuquerque
The Fall of Optimum House
The Lonesome Autocrat
Tracking Backward
Turn the Joker Around
Reaching Checkmate

Available at www.amazon.com,
www.barnesandnoble.com
and other vendors.

www.ingramcontent.com/pod-product-compliance
Lightning Source LLC
Chambersburg PA
CBHW032044240626
47154CB00003B/1073